THE CITY
of SEALIONS

EVA SALLIS was born in Bendigo. She has an MA in literature and a PhD in comparative literature from The University of Adelaide. Eva won the 1997 *The Australian*/Vogel literary award for her first novel, *Hiam*. She lives near Port Adelaide.

ALSO BY EVA SALLIS

Hiam (1998)
Sheherazade through the Looking Glass:
The Metamorphosis of the 1001 Nights (1999)

THE CITY
of SEALIONS

EVA SALLIS

ALLEN & UNWIN

First published in 2002

 This book has been assisted by the Government of South Australia through Arts South Australia.

Allen & Unwin
83 Alexander Street
Crows Nest NSW 2065
Australia
Phone: (61 2) 8425 0100
Fax: (61 2) 9906 2218
Email: info@allenandunwin.com
Web: www.allenandunwin.com

National Library of Australia
Cataloguing-in-Publication entry:

Sallis, E.K. (Eva K.).
     The city of sealions.

ISBN 1 86508 617 7.

     1. Australians — Yemen — Fiction. 2. Racially mixed children — Fiction. 3. Mothers and daughters — Fiction. I. Title.

A823.3

Set in 10.75/15 pt Scala by Asset Typesetting Pty Ltd
Printed in Australia by the McPherson's Printing Group

10 9 8 7 6 5 4 3 2 1

For Roger
Face to the salt spray and a wild sea

CONTENTS

PROLOGUE

On the first night in Yemen, Lian dreamed of the beach.
A wind was up, blowing in from the Arctic seasummer
which shimmered on the horizon. Her feet stepped out
of the water, unmaking their splashes. The dream ran
backwards, the sea leaping up to suck the wet from her
legs, to grab her feet in cushioned calm. The puffed and
murky sand in the shallows swirled like genies back into
bottles, calming into smooth, clear ripples around her
soles. Yellow-eyed fish with a thin stripe of silver inside
their translucent bodies rushed panicked towards her
toes, converging into clusters. Waves picked themselves
up, tidied the mess and slurped like withdrawn tongues
back into the ocean. She wanted to swim but the sea was
belching up rotten ships and repairing them. The *Norma*
shot up stern first from the shipping channel, spilling

silver whiting like fireworks. The ships looked like old crones. Not all their parts and components could be found. Bits of the *John Robb* huddled together in a shiply shape. The horizon was jagged with black hulks, swarming with seaweed-draped people dancing on the decks. The beautiful *Zanoni*, the *Perth*. The *Sydney*. The *Lusitania* and the *Titanic* arm in arm, listing. Korean Airbus 007. The sea was becoming very crowded. Trumpets played and singing voices floated in on the hot wind. The sand rushed to calm all disturbances.

A drowned sailor at her feet slowly lost his greenish hue and his buttons shed their barnacles. Crabs scuttled towards her, sideways.

Phi-Van passed by in a goldrush coolie hat, paddling a coracle. She waved and blew a foghorn out of a small trumpet.

Lian woke. *Allahu Akbar* — The call to prayer swelled into the still night near and far, as unsynchronised as the crowing of roosters. Dogs in the street below barked and yelped, fighting or playing. The darkness was alive with other wild sounds she could not comprehend.

WATER

Lian was born on an island less than one hundred kilometres in length, a tiny dot in the windy blue south of the world, one of the last pieces of hot, dry gold before the globe is a deep and frozen white. Lian's home was sea-rimmed, sea-circled. Her sun rose every morning out of the sea and set behind the mallee. The Island was a mere scar in that seething, shimmering skin. The sea shuddered with big creatures gliding silently, weightless in the translucent blue: great simultaneously veering schools of silver trevally, sand-grazing whiting, pulse of warmth from the passing dolphins; and the sea shook with small creatures shooting from them in flashes of light, in streamers of fear. The fried earth and the gold grasses ran down the slopes to end in the crescent sands, bones and twisted driftwood of the shore. Wherever Lian went she could see an airborne haze of salt water and smell its purity and its rot. Dry deaths lay about on land, the roadkill desiccated in days in summer; and rich wet deaths popped in small explosions, like burst red grapes spilling a moment of red into the blue ocean.

She was a reserved and independent child, a little strange, good at swimming, fishing and diving, the joy of her parents' hearts. She lived for her father, for fish and the sea. She endured school, enjoyed or endured home and then fished, cushioned, the unstable skin ceaselessly breaking and mending around her.

The wind tore over the land, so filled with sea spray that it seemed to have been blown from the mouth of the ocean.

Their house was a typical South Australian settler's cottage with sandstone walls and a front verandah extended like a hand held stiffly at the brow, shading the eyes from the glare. The verandah rose to a high roof at the front, sloping away to a low roof at the back which could be reached by Nev's fingertips, under which the tiny kitchen, washhouse and bathroom were squeezed. There were four main rooms and a small lean-to tacked on the side next to Nev and Phi-Van's room. The floors were polished wood, the yellow of goats' eyes, and the furniture was all either blackwood dressers and cabinets inherited from Nev's great-grandmother or sturdy raw-wood boxes and tables made by Nev. The house usually shone with Phi-Van's attentions and smelt of sea spray, lemongrass and coriander.

The small family had no friends, although the islanders were friendly and Nev's family had lived there for generations. They did have Nev's brother Mal, his wife Claire, and Lian's cousins. Nev and Mal did their best to make sure that Lian belonged, that she was proud of being an Islander and an Australian.

'You're as Aussie as they come and don't you forget it.' Nev points his cigarette at her quiet little seven-year-old self and then stubs it on his boot. 'Your family's been farming and fishing on this island for more than a hundred years. And before that they were always island-livin' and seafarin' people.'

'What about Phi-Van?'

'Phi-Van's a silkie. She came from the sea.' Nev waves with expansive inaccuracy at the Great Southern Ocean. 'So she's one of us too.'

'You're so like your mother,' Mal says to Lian's flouncing teenage self.

Lian is irritated. The one person in the world she most differs from is her mother.

'A slope, you mean,' she sneers.

Mal is impervious.

'Nup. Nev's more slope than you, have you looked at

him lately? I meant that you're both mean and nasty buggers with a hell of a stubborn exterior. You've got the motherlode running through ya, but Nev and some other poor bloke're gunna be mining away for life before they see a glimpse of it. Can tell it's there, but. Metal detectors.' He taps his head at the temple.

And Lian stalks off.

Phi-Van did come from the sea but Nev found her on the mainland, in the city. He met her on the street outside Adelaide Magistrates Court where he was defending his bees' right to swarm on a fire hydrant. It was her first day on a protection visa. On impulse, Nev took the bone-thin silent girl with scars and liquid black hair home with him. And she followed because she did not think she could take one more second on the street with no English and impaled by eyes. Nev was the only option that presented itself. She learned English slowly in the easy company of Nev's family and married Nev ten years later.

Mal was a farmer, at ease with the land he farmed and the animals he tended, birthed, shaved and shot. He was good with dogs. He was the older brother and had stayed with the farm, although Nev looked after the nomadic beehives, moving them from district to district. The farm was too sparse, too drought-ridden a place to support the families of two sons. Nev, Phi-Van and Lian went there for every harvest, every shearing, every festival and every excuse. Without them the meagre pickings from wheat and sheep and bees could not even have kept Mal, Claire and Lian's three cousins.

And so Nev had walked around on the seabed in gumboots, doing contract work, on and off, for as long as Lian could remember. His work world ebbed and flowed with old oil and sewage. Encased head to toe in a tatty grey and black wetsuit, he trailed a hookah air line through the murky waters of the harbour, hooking props, ship or ferry bolts and anchors to a chain, to be winched up and repaired in the stark dry air. Once, just after she had learned to dive, he took Lian down with him. She stared up the hulls, keels reaching down like upside down skyscrapers, each heavier and more solid overhead than a thundercloud. Boats loomed in the dim light like a fleet of starships. The green sand beneath was brittle with dead things. Nev's eyes were crinkled behind his mask. He winked at her as gobs of purple grease drifted away from his hands. She floated and cavorted around him like Tinkerbell, dwarfed by the hulks, her green fluoro fins bright in the dim light.

Nev Seawalker. Bravest and, if he didn't have to wear a mask, handsomest man on the seabed.

Their house had a worn grey patch in the wooden floor stretching from the door in a V down the hallway. Years of Nev's wet and salty boots and Lian's sandy feet had rubbed away the varnish and the golden colour. Phi-Van covered it with mats, periodically; but the salt and weather whirled into the house by her husband and daughter still soaked through and wore away the floor.

Lian was not allowed in Phi-Van's room, which was a dressing room, perhaps once a sunroom, accessed through French doors from her parents' bedroom. It was where Phi-Van dressed and retreated if she needed to. Nev called it her boodwa and made a game of it, but something in the way he winked showed Lian that for him it was not funny. Phi-Van could be swallowed by her boodwa for days and, when Lian was very small, the room seemed to have an unpredictable, even malicious appetite.

Inside, it had a small camp bed, a dresser and a wardrobe which was locked. It was always darkened with red curtains and reminded Lian of a picture of a man living in the belly of a whale. She imagined her mother in there, reading, writing a journal and chewing the raw fish that the whale accidentally swallowed.

Nev, Phi-Van and Lian were, until Lian was five, the long-term marooned, self-sufficient from the world and dependent on each other. Seated around the waxed gold-wood table in the sunny kitchen of the cottage, they were an eccentric unit, hardy and remote, as if this was the only cottage ever built and they the only people on the Island. The few signs of human industry — tins containing utensils on the shelves and the spear gun in the corner — were perhaps found objects washed up from far away, found beachcombing or on the seafloor. Nev had waited, fishing, and the sea had even brought him a wife from another world, still faintly blistered from five months in an open boat and much too calm. Lian herself appeared as if from the blue, landing ashore from her mother's body in a rush of water and blood.

They sit around the table for breakfast, silent. Lian is a small, wiry child with the beauty of form and wild grace that some children have at five. Her legs are kicking and twirling under the table, twining and parting, flicking and swinging. She has bright brown eyes that dart from Nev to Phi-Van and back as if waiting for something to happen for which she is ready. Her mouth is slightly open. Phi-Van moves the honey pot away from her extended hand and Lian doesn't complain. Phi-Van is raising the child with precision and without the help of her own mother, and, so long as Lian gets three or four meals a day, Nev doesn't interfere. Lian eats what Phi-Van did as a child, as far as Phi-Van can recall, and planning Lian's food in the correct amounts takes almost all her energy.

Outside sounds — bees from the hives in the sea garden, distant surf, spur-winged plovers — fill the kitchen until the rising hiss of a kettle drowns them out. Phi-Van gets up and goes to the stove but the kettle isn't there. Lian cackles and caws like a plover five times. She is answered by the bird in the dunes. Nev chuckles and slides the honey to Lian and Phi-Van cuffs them both and grins, her pale face momentarily as lit and joyous as Lian's. Phi-Van takes the honey away to the sound of angry bees. Nev grabs her with his big hands fitting almost all the way around her waist and, although Phi-Van pulls away, Lian can tell that her mother likes it. Lian is suddenly in a state of rare delight and begins jumping in her chair, crowing.

'She *will* have to go to school,' Phi-Van says suddenly, and the bees stop. The plover calls from the dunes, but Lian doesn't answer. Phi-Van is looking across to Nev, her face strained and afraid.

'So she will,' Nev says, as though he has never considered this. Lian's eyes plead with him for a moment but then her face becomes impassive and her expression unfathomable.

Lian felt watched from her earliest memory and performed every action with the onlooker in mind. Every word she uttered she first considered how it sounded and what effect it would have on Phi-Van. And being so careful, weighing everything in what she imagined to be the mind of her mother, stunted something in Lian.

Until she went to school, Lian slept in a cot in the room opposite that of her parents, with the door ajar so that they could hear her. She fought to stay awake. Once asleep, she knew she would feel Phi-Van as a shadow in the room, watching her, and, night after night, she would struggle like a fly in honey to wake and drive the shadow out. There was nothing soothing about the presence of her mother in the darkness. At nightfall, or by moonlight, it was no longer Phi-Van in the room, but whatever it was that Phi-Van carried with her, darkening their lives. Once, she had managed to drag herself from sleep and, sticky and afraid, she had *seen* something else in the room. She screamed, in a continuous ever-billowing terror, begging Phi-Van to help her. And her mother, eyes like holes, had stared at Lian as if *she* was the thing in the room. Shaking and shuddering, Phi-Van backed slowly away from those echoing screams, out of the door and shut it behind her. She then rushed down to the shore for Nev, who was salmon fishing. It was the only time she had ever been to the beach.

Lian forgot the source of her night terrors but never asked Phi-Van for help again. And she knew that Phi-Van could not stand screaming, even happy screeches. 'Too chirpy for oldies!' Nev would say, wincing and holding his ears before Phi-Van could leave the room. Lian wasn't fooled. Nev shouted, hooted and squealed himself when they were alone, out fishing.

As Lian grew she became increasingly remote. She loved Nev, Phi-Van, the birds and the fish, the shimmering gold land and the cool, shaken silk of the sea. And she was far from cold-hearted. Contact with her heart was simply delayed. Experiences had to wait in her head, be frisked and analysed, admired and replayed, before they ever had access to her heart.

People said she was even-tempered, calm, *very Asiatic*. Her mother said she was cold, but that was only frustration. Her father said she was trim and ocean-going, *rigged with a storm staysail*, and could ride out a hurricane. But Lian's was not the kind of reserve that seems cool and collected. Anyone who watched her closely would soon get the sense that every movement was half made, every sound half its strength, every gesture curtailed. She gave the impression of being bound into stillness, of having intense, even frightening energy but working within invisible restrictions. Children were far better at noticing this than adults and avoided her the way some animals avoid the injured or sick.

A seagull is bobbing in the waves, sated, looking like a small seaworthy vessel: unsinkable. Squalling seagulls dive all around it into the fry, making small professional splashes as they hit the water, to rise almost immediately on their sail-wings, twisting, gulping, fighting and diving again. Suddenly the bobbing form of the bird falls awkwardly, wings splayed on the surface of the water, yanked downwards like the floater on a gar line. Its bill ducks forward and it flaps messily against a hidden anchor, catching itself in the net of the viscous surface, holding hard to the aerial realm — all just for a split second. It rises suddenly into the air, shambling, frightened. Lian sees two drops of blood fall from tiny orange stumps, fall slowly and sail in an arc on the wind until they hit the water and cloud the blue momentarily, then vanish. Just two. She loses the bird in the indifferent flock. Then she sees it hovering in even, conservative strokes on the breeze, two red stains marking its crisp white undercarriage.

It reminds her of herself.

She is twelve.

Lian could not be close to her mother. Nev said that Lian had struggled to get out and away, with no thought of herself or her mother, from the moment of conception. Phi-Van had had, he said, a shocker of a pregnancy. Then, for twelve months following Lian's birth, Phi-Van had been unable to touch her tiny daughter. She had hovered, solicitous and pale, outside the circle of Nev's big hands wrapped around the tiny naked ribcage. She had washed nappies and cleaned the room feverishly, staring through the bars of the cot. She had sniffed the air over the baby, pacing up and down for Nev to change her. She had rocked Lian to sleep. Nev had done all the rest, and yet Phi-Van's eyes had been bright with a possessive jealousy throughout.

When Phi-Van began to touch Lian, her daughter evaded her, wriggling, twisting away, laughing unhappily. Phi-Van touched Lian's body with a kind of suppressed lust. When Phi-Van touched she was feeling for Lian's future — always with the distracted expression she had tapping a watermelon, pressing an avocado or a mango — half imagining the family she had lost and the family she could regain. Children know when a touch is wrong. Lian, touched with tainted mother-love, enjoyed no touch, not even from Nev, unless it was in play-fighting.

As Lian grew, Phi-Van drove her daughter from her with a strange cruelty but also clung to her with a suffocating and insatiable desperation. It was as if Lian was her life raft.

And Lian? Lian didn't hate her mother. But she drew a magic circle around herself as soon as she was old enough to realise that Phi-Van's desire would never rest. It was a dragon coiled in Phi-Van's belly which drove the mother to rummage in the body and soul of her daughter for something she had misplaced. Lian could not give her mother anything without it costing everything so she resolutely gave nothing. Lian offered her mother a cold and immobile face or a spiky warmth which was expressed in contorted, rapid and dismissive gestures of what could only be a sneaking affection and longing for approval. Nev watched them both, mildly spooked by how similar they were.

Nev was loving to both his wife and daughter, bewildered by their antagonism. He could have smoked and yarned and watched them both all day, if they would only let up at each other and get on with being mellow like him. He stood between his wife and his daughter, not to separate them but to force them to stay together for as long as he could.

'We're all in the same boat here,' he pleaded and Phi-Van immediately allied herself with him.

'Can't we just be a normal family, just this Christmas, without someone getting the blues?' he pleaded and Lian backed him up, almost vindictively.

Lian's eyes flicked from parent to parent.

'She'll study Vietnamese!' Phi-Van's voice was breathless on the last high syllable, and, like all her statements, it almost sounded as if it was a question. Her eyes glittered, staring at Nev as though he could make or break Lian's interest in Vietnamese. Her cheeks were flushed.

'Where would she use it?' Nev said easily, not really paying attention, picking at mud on his jeans.

Phi-Van went white as suddenly as a startled octopus and Lian held her breath. Nev looked up.

'Well, Fi-Fi, there aren't many Vietnamese-speakers around. And you speak English.'

Phi-Van said something, rapidly, with a rocking, liquid rhythm, in Vietnamese. Nev and Lian stared at her. Phi-Van kept talking at their blank faces until Nev got up and wrapped his arms around her tightly, shaking his head, murmuring, 'Best forgotten, love, all that stuff, best forgotten,' and winking at Lian over her mother's shoulder.

Lian walked to the beach, her heart pounding. She didn't like Nev's wink. She didn't like Phi-Van's transformed face when she spoke angry Vietnamese at them. She kicked up the sand with her bare toes, staring out at the whitecaps glittering in the crisp autumn sunlight. Her private image of Phi-Van, born out of the sea, riding in naked on a giant shell to meet Nev on the shore, smiling, long black hair streaming and with blossom in her hair, was shaken. She wished there had been no before. And she swore to herself that she would *never never never* learn Vietnamese.

It was impossible to be angry about anything if the experience stamped and stormed and dissipated itself in the antechamber; if heated faces and loud words cooled and eventually had to blow into their hands before a hearing. For many years Lian was proud of herself in the afterglow of the praise of others. When people said she was *mature and so collected*, she saw herself as a trim and admirable entity, more alone and complete and altogether less messy than others. When people said she was *sweet and even-tempered*, she felt herself gliding on the words, floating as the sweet must, for they are above all cruelty and vice. And when people said she was *a perfect angel*, she knew that in some sense this was absolutely true. They were, after all, saying that she was not like other people, not human: that she was free of the turmoil of the insatiable and the lazy wisdom of the mellow.

'Wear a dress, Lian. You don't want your uncle to mistake you for a boy.'

'Stupid,' muttered Lian. Then louder, 'As if he would!'

'You are fat now, but if you don't even try to be feminine, you will be fat and ugly always. You have the arms of a boy, look!' Phi-Van's voice rose, and she poked Lian's stringy forearm with a white finger. Lian twisted away, grinning. She liked her muscles and her strength, and she liked Phi-Van to notice but always felt an obscure, even pleasurable shame when Phi-Van did.

She didn't want to be boy-like, but even whales knew her sex, so she didn't believe a word Phi-Van said about it.

Once, diving, she had seen the water darken to the west, as if clouds were rolling in underwater — at an impossible speed, for clouds. Huge shadows formed and flowed towards her. Southern right whales. A calf and two adults. The child hung at the flank of its mother, who cruised steadily towards Lian and then slowly veered, rolling, passing in a long, slow spaceship manoeuvre, greeting her eye to eye. A gentle glance, from the mother, from her child, and then they became watery storm clouds again and were gone.

'If you'da been a boy, she wouldn've come near, not with a calf so young,' Nev said, flicking cigarette ash into the wind with the gesture of an expert on whales. Lian, eleven years old, had felt downright sexy, privileged. She put her hand on her hip, moved her rib cage a little sideways and extended a skinny leg. It was the start of her curiosity about others' mothers.

Later, she wasn't sure if she believed Nev either. Phi-Van spoke to upset her and Nev to cheer her up, and so they cancelled each other out.

Lian had a suspicious mind.

Nev told Lian that ever since she had arrived on the Island, Phi-Van had had to have her tiny suitcase packed and waiting in the wardrobe. Lian had been through it, secretively, having picked the lock with some fencing wire. It had odd things in it: amidst a very few ordinary clothes and a pair of high-heeled shoes, it had superglue, a packet of Anchor brown sugar, Lian's first haircut, a square of cotton material with a faded pink floral print, an airline blindfold, Phi-Van's wedding dress, a child's sunhat, a newspaper clipping which called her a 'Sole-Survivor' and 'Island's First Viet-Bride', a sheet of folded yellow beeswax, a filleting knife, an ear of wheat, twenty packets of tampons, several prescriptions worth of sleeping tablets, a raincoat, a wad of money hidden in the collar of the raincoat, and a tissue full of Nev's nail parings.

Lian entered the house stealthily, as always. She held her breath and kept her steps soundless until she had worked out where her mother was. Phi-Van was asleep on the living room rug, twitching and whimpering softly. Lian crept up and squatted beside her mother, watching the pale face, caught by the strange piping and mewling Phi-Van emitted now and then. Phi-Van's face flickered with inner shadows like a dim lamp with a butterfly trapped inside. She was pearlescent and soft, even gentle or vulnerable looking. Her long black hair was coiled under her head and neck, shining in the afternoon light. Lian could smell the faint perfume rising from it. Phi-Van's troubled hands closed and opened. They were almost pure ivory, fine, long fingered, elegant. Lian laid her own next to them. Hers were broad like Nev's and already the same size as Phi-Van's. Lian lay down too, face to face, and then, softly, softly, extended a leg and placed it between Phi-Van's arms. Phi-Van gripped it tight to her chest and the whimpering stopped. Lian thought for a moment to pull out of the clutching, twining arms but then suddenly liked it and surrendered, giving all of that leg and adjusting her body so that she was not tugging at it in the least. Their breathing levelled together. Phi-Van's arms heated her salty leg and she began to glow with the warmth as it travelled through her. She was about to close her eyes when Phi-Van breathed in beyond their unison beat and yawned, drawing her lips back from her teeth, and Lian, caught in that yellowing doorway, felt her heart race and the sweat suddenly prickle on her trapped leg. Then the mouth closed and the eyes opened, staring straight into Lian's. They were glazed and unlit. Lian ripped her leg from the now unresisting arms, leaping back and away. She ran from the house.

When Lian was twelve years old, something happened in their small, storm-swept household which was bigger than the ocean cyclone Nev and Lian had ridden out the spring before and more bitter at the core than any of the other confusing memories which mother and daughter packed into their separate satchels, neatly folded and bound, necessary but forgotten in the press of the layers above. The effect was at first cataclysmic but it was the invisible after-effects which were the most destructive. This event corroded away Lian's equanimity.

Lian and Nev went to the mainland for a holiday. It was an impromptu trip which began when she walked in, dripping on the wooden floor, and Nev said, 'Let's go to Adelaide for the fireworks.' She made her eyes big at him, whooped and stripped out of her bathers as she ran to get ready. They were halfway across Baxters Passage, leaning on the rail of the ferry together and staring out to sea for whales, when Lian remembered Phi-Van.

'We forgot to tell Phi-Van,' she said, clapping a hand over her mouth and staring wide-eyed at Nev.

'Nah. She's in hospital in Adelaide waiting for us,' Nev said, still staring out to sea.

Lian was silent, digesting this. She had thought Phi-Van was locked in her room since ... Wednesday. It was Saturday. She shrugged, as if to say, 'Oh, I knew *that*', annoyed at being caught out not knowing.

They still went to the fireworks for Australia Day.

The rockets sliced through the velvet summer sky and flowered over the riverbank, the lights plunging vertiginously downward in the still, black reflection. The roaring murmur of the crowd. The tinnitus whisper of ten thousand transistors. The cries of the children egged on by the loudspeaker —

'Blooooooooooooooooo!'

'Reeeeeeeeeed!'

'Blue! Blooooooooooooooooooo!'

Looking down, Lian almost couldn't tell which world was which. The darkness on the riverbank rustled with shuffling bodies, muffled chatter and the breathing of children. As the invisible and faintly whistling bombs rose high, the river and the sky were black but stained at the centre with orange smoke. Then, when the blue or red bursts spread like anemones and lit up the faces in almost submarine silence, water and sky were red, blue, gold, the mirror images holding still, for a moment, like the hands of dancers almost touching for a measured pause. The twin worlds flamed in unison, the voices rose in a wave and then the explosions came to earth and crashed in a roar and crackle more sharp than surf.

And Lian forgot completely about Phi-Van.

On the way back from Adelaide after the fireworks, Nev bought Phi-Van a small dog, a silky terrier puppy. Why, no-one was able later to say, least of all Nev. It was a tiny dog, a *nonsense*, according to Uncle Mal, and Lian agreed. They were all used to the bold bodies of exuberant kelpie puppies, larger at birth than this windblown mite of black fur. Lian loved puppies and dogs, something she and Mal shared, but she touched this diminutive creature with cautious, self-conscious hands. Nev grinned and said he got it because it was different, and in fact it must have been something felt in a surge and acted on with motor reflex. As if to emphasise its difference, the tiny beast turned gold and silver almost overnight: gold around the face and saddled with lank, steadily lengthening silver hair, grandmother hair that, on a dog, was strangely lovely to look at and touch. Once this gold and silver object with eyes was ensconced, Mal could only look at it and shake his head. It had an intelligent if puppy-silly face which spun to watch whoever was talking from its position on Phi-Van's lap. It shivered, too — somehow overanimate.

The astounding thing was that Phi-Van, who hated dogs, loved it. She came home two days after Nev and Lian and didn't go to her room and hide. Nev's voice leapt in his throat with happiness throughout a golden summer as Phi-Van bowed over the small, serious dog, her hard white face soft and flushed. Nev leapt on the inside and Mal shook his head in wonder; but that was not all. Lian was watching, too, with something more like horror than warmth or wonder. She saw something that Nev knew about Phi-Van but she did not recognise.

She saw a person she had never seen or met before, curved over a creature. She saw five-fingered caresses, the new scars on wrists flaming; she saw a tender, even moist eye; a cloak wrapped around a small body in the wind; a secret sharing of food; and felt two warm patches on a pillow. She missed nothing. And each touch that alighted on the small body of the young dog made her more attentive.

What happened at the end of summer set in place the cold war between Lian and Phi-Van and solidified a quiet and vicious antagonism, filled with pain and hatred from both sides. Its territory was Lian's body, which Lian shored up to be impenetrable and Phi-Van battered savagely with her hungry love, disappointment and unhappiness.

It was Nev who found the body of the dog, after two days of Phi-Van's tormented eyes and warmth already receding. It was bound like a mummy in many layers of cloth torn from a sheet, its legs bent back so that it almost looked like a small human baby. Only its nose was visible but it was bound too tightly to have been able to breathe even for a few seconds.

When Phi-Van reappeared out of the boodwa two weeks later, Lian's body greeted her by bursting out in fistulous sores. When Phi-Van noticed, she grabbed Lian by the hand, dragged her to her room and ordered her to undress. She planted Lian naked in front of her, seeking out each sore and dabbing it with a sticky ointment, murmuring softly all the while on her daughter's ugliness. Her daughter was marked for unhappiness, for a single life, for barrenness; no-one would want this scarred rag once the red rage of the sores died down. 'Look, look!' she said, shaking Lian if Lian's eyes wandered away from her face. Lian's body stung and burned all over and her skin shrank under Phi-Van's touch.

Phi-Van walked out to get some old clothes to cover the greasy skin and Lian stared down at herself. The arms and legs were spotted with weeping sores and the chest was swathed in fiery welts. The tiny nipples were like symmetrical reddened scars and the narrow hip bones protruded. She could feel that red spots reached up the neck to her ears and riddled her scalp but her face was smooth. The faint unpleasant smell of suppuration was masked now by the sickly, invasive smell of the ointment Phi-Van's thumb had pressed into her. She sagged, letting the knees sway back in their flexible joints and pushing the belly out beyond the ribs. She had seen her body reflected in Phi-Van's eyes, her ugliness in Phi-Van's pursed lips. What monstrous skin! What a creeping, evil thing she lived in! She would try to have nothing to do with it again. She hoped it would shrivel up and go away. Phi-Van never spoke about her, Lian, but only about her body and she suddenly felt glad that her body hurt and looked horrible.

The eczema faded and left no scars.

And although Nev must have understood somehow, he looked at Lian differently now and then, and Lian, being a child deluged with once-frozen fears, blamed Phi-Van as much as she could for the ripple of change in her father.

She had basked in the praise of others and had felt invincible in her armour, but after the death of Phi-Van's dog she slowly imploded. Outwardly, nothing changed. On the inside the idea that she was *not as she seemed* ate her away. When she came home from school, the scant sea garden sighed, not with but against her, and she noticed for the first time that the sunlight across the floorboards of the hallway seemed to bar her passage.

Nev's silence, Phi-Van's absence, the grass, the sunlight and the sea all said she was the keeper of the secret, and that it was a great scarring crime. She had no means of knowing why she had killed the dog — so slowly, so dreamily, so calmly. She could not even recall the peace she felt or that love had played a part. But she could place the acid of others' reactions inside her and question what it meant.

She looked into her heart and told herself that she now knew herself for what she really was.

And she noticed her detachment.

She realised that other people felt things without delay. She stared out at a stormy ocean, flattened and beaten to slags and streamers of foam, too rough or ragged for surfing, and realised that the sea was more like her mother than herself. And the ocean was messy and uneven and vicious. She saw clearly that she, Lian, was unnaturally still. That something in her was broken, or not connected, and had been so from her earliest years.

After due consideration, Lian became sad.

Had she listened and told stories only because she could have none of her own? Her adventures at sea, the day she caught her first snapper, alone in the tinny, retold with appropriate gesticulations and excitement to Nev and Phi-Van, seemed to be a way to have an experience which, *at the time*, she had only observed. She had known, with an anticipatory frisson, that this was going to be a good one when it went through due procedure, but at the time, as the jewelled red form of the giant fish, as its iridescent eye, hot blue dorsal dots, fine-fingered coral fins, and mermaid tail were wrestled over the gunwale, bleeding down the shaft of the gaff, *she had felt nothing.*

Her sadness became so constant that after a time she caught up with it and felt sad when she was sad, even if she was a day or two out of synchronisation. Under its influence every moment in her short life in which she had cried in rage and misery stood out in stark relief to her. Her earliest memory was of glittering insect-filled morning grasses as high as her chest, tossed all around her by a light breeze that ruffled her hair, fingered her face — the world shining and shaking around her — and her standing with her hands at her sides, desolate. She probed these memories when once she had toyed, with casual pleasure, with praise and the words of others. These memories were formed in the shadow of the thing that was missing, the thing that had no name or story, and through them Lian could sense absence. Soon, for she was fourteen and singularly obsessional, she noticed that every experience had been the torment of not feeling. Not feeling the dawn. Not feeling the sea smashing against her face and rolling her like a dead puppy to return her again and again to the shore.

She learned to be a vulture. If she could not have her experiences, she could prey upon them afterwards. Her experiences were felt, known, understood, enjoyed afterwards. She became the master of a carrion intro-spection.

Lian only ever cried after having pictured herself crying.

Lian became a collector of stories. When she was very young she made stories of her own experiences in order to experience them (with the pleasurable bonus of then being able to tell them well). Then, in her teens, she began to collect the stories of others, became the voyeur, the analyst of others' lives. She collected sad and happy stories, vignettes and longer narratives. She became observant and even thought herself clever. Some stories she wrote down and some she remembered, almost satisfied that she was proving the warmth of her character by demonstrating it in her stories, in her close observations of people and in her benignity with their secrets. By the time she was fifteen she knew more of the terrible stories and the sufferings of the families on the Island than any other person, even the priest. People trusted her stillness, or ignored her. She looked so *Asiatic* and was after all a *child* and for some reason that was enough for her to eavesdrop on conversations and altercations from which she would otherwise have been barred. She knew, better than anyone, how to link up fragments found at church, school and in the supermarket and see the shadow they cast and hinted at. She was a silent and aloof teenager, *a good girl*, and knowledge made her feel powerful.

She neither wrote down Phi-Van's story nor collected it in her head. She armoured herself in stories to protect herself from it.

When Lian was fifteen, she discovered the church youth group; or, rather, they discovered her. She sang descants and harmonies to their songs and they congratulated themselves on a find. That broad and mellow voice, with its range of lights and shadows, was unexpected, and the group leader could see the potential of such surprise, for, he told himself, *Asians are not singers.* She was a little miracle. It was a pity she was so tall.

For a short while Lian was happy. She sang, believing in their love for each other and for her. The spirit of charity and acceptance, the sprinkler system for the dissemination of love amongst the brothers and the sisters, calmed her and seemed to her most beautiful. She sang, elated, grateful, making her harmonies expressive of the rapture she glimpsed in their company.

The church organised activity nights in youth-group leaders' houses. The thought of hours and hours of food and song and prayer with her new family hovered in her mind, illuminating everything she did. She tried to do churchy things. She read the Bible instead of diving, imagining the others in their rooms scattered over the Island, reading with her, perhaps the same verse; perhaps, miraculously, the same words.

The night came round. John picked up a pile of kids in his panel van, roaring along the dirt roads praising the Lord and playing 'Jesus Christ Superstar' and 'I'm Gonna Hammer Out Love' on the stereo. They sang along, raucously, joyously, rubbing and jostling against each other in the back. Karen put her arms around Lian and hugged her tight.

The leader's house was lit up and welcoming. There was food, people, prayer, warmth. The three plastic trays set at equidistant points around the room were continually replenished with tuna sandwich fingers made of crustless Tip Top white bread of melt in the mouth softness. The jugs of Cottees orange cordial were endlessly refilled. Lian, not usually fed white bread or cordial or, for that matter, canned tuna, became hyperactive and overjoyed.

They played games. Karen put a blindfold on Lian and spun her around. She had to find the people (who didn't run from her) and, feeling their faces, with the Lord's help, name them. She got them all right, and Karen hugged her a second time and whispered in her ear, 'You're one of us, now!'

After dinner a seventeen-year-old boy named Randy gave a serious speech about how he found the love of Christ in his life and was born again. Lian thought about anemones and cuttlefish. If you were lucky enough to pass near Christ you changed colour. You flowered and got fed, or blended in and gained protection. 'Praise the Lord,' she murmured. Everyone in the room praised the Lord. Randy was talking about miracles and the room became turbulent. People near Lian began to sweat and murmur more loudly. Then Randy said, 'Let us pray.' Instead of lowering his head and mumbling demurely into his chest, he stood tall and raised his face to the exposed beams of the ceiling and began howling his prayer to God. The leader stood next to him with one hand on Randy's shoulder and the other raised in the air as a conduit. Everyone around Lian stood up and began praying loudly. Lian tried to think of everything for which she should praise the Lord and loudly exclaimed the details of each one as it came to mind. Thank you Lord for the sea anemones and the hermit crabs. The room changed again and she was sure she could hear sobbing. The cacophony of prayer became chaotic. Next to her Karen fell to her knees and began burbling in a foreign tongue. Lian looked at her friend's closed eyes in horror. Even she could tell this was no real language. It had no pattern, no repeat in difference: only repetition of the burble the tongue could manage waggling freely. At that moment Randy gave a falsetto cry and fell face forward to the floor, saved from a blood nose by the leader who eased him down and then left him there, raising his own face to the beams and praying words Lian couldn't lip-read. All around her people began shrieking and sighing, each speaking a language invented as they went and unique to their tongue's flailing capacities. Lian felt very lonely. Each was proud of reaching privacy with God and joining the elect who had no real need of each other. She too felt heightened and charged, and felt it was quite right to be crying. Through her tears she found herself, some-what guiltily, disbelieving everything. She longed for the sea.

She never went back to youth group. They prayed for her for several months but she was lost.

Lian made an inventory of her experiences, calculated their life expectancies, plotted their charts and kept them on file. Through her inventory she was able to know herself, to know her likely response to a given situation and manufacture herself at need. She was able to appear as a participant in life before her feelings or reactions manifested themselves. Sometimes they took her by surprise but more often she felt as if she had already experienced them, and the difference between the real feelings and the theatre of actors became, over time, blurred. Lian became slightly happier as she entered her late teens and resolutely suppressed consciousness of her delayed feelings and their biographers who played the roles in public. She had, by then, the burning inward focus of the self-obsessed, the mark of the damaged, of those who huddle around a volatile cancer, careful not to jolt it. She was not able to love without feeling a fraud so she shut herself safely away from love.

At eighteen Lian is a tall girl stalking around university for orientation at the beginning of first year. Her smooth, tawny face has the faintest hunted expression tinged with a sliding fear or perhaps evasiveness. Her long legs and purposeful stride have a scuttle to them, and her straight, sinewy body also has a faint shielded look. Her rich voice is sometimes so low it cannot be heard. She plays sport, runs, works out savagely and with little pleasure, as a means to keep herself lean. She has spent a couple of years trying to be everything that Phi-Van could want but allowing her mother no bit of herself. She is lean and beautiful and accepted into medicine but has enrolled in arts and, with some inner joy, is taking her lovely body away from the Island to live in a flat and thrash it with junk food. She is powerful — and cruel with it. She revels in the thought that she is unscarred by the long cold war, that Phi-Van would rend her limb from limb but cannot: that she is the victor.

She climbed the stairs to the library, watching the jeans-clad legs, crotches and thighs on the steps above her, wishing she hadn't worn jeans. What if someone was subjecting her bum to the same analytical gaze that she was using? What if her cut, her straightlegs did that, or that, to her bum? Her cheeks burned slightly and she decided to get two full-length mirrors for the flat. At the top of the stairs she adjusted her jeans and shirt in quick unconscious movements.

Arabic caught her by surprise at the library door. She might even have studied Vietnamese in order to not speak it to Phi-Van. But something caught her eye — a dark, curving, cresting line, a stylised stormy ocean obliterating half-sunk masts stretched across the centre of a poster. It was enough to hook her. *ARABIC*, the header said, in a mystery-of-the-East font. *Study the language of the Koran and the Arabian Nights! Arabic is the official language of 22 countries and is spoken in 16 more. From beginners level, no prerequisites.* And Lian enrolled in Arabic because she knew nothing about it.

Lian left the Island when she was eighteen in search of a foster mother tongue which could give voice to her own story, and then left the great southern land when she was twenty-three, following Arabic as far as it could take her.

Arabia Felix. Happy Arabia. The far and forbidden land, the green roof of the world, the land of myrrh and frankincense, the cradle of coffee, was named *happy* by northerners who, in some hyperborean dream, believed in a blessed land in the deep south. Lian's passport was in her pocket, her bags in the hold, as the domestic flight from Adelaide to Melbourne sailed over the shore of the last continent at a steep angle, tipped its wing at the golden rim of the Island, and turned away.

Eight disoriented Muslim men circled hesitantly at sunset in a deserted corner of Melbourne airport. They stared at the sky and at their feet. They settled, faced Tasmania and prayed, prostrating themselves to the south. Outside the thick glass, planes glimmered in the fiery sky and, silent as butterflies, rose and descended.

Lian's journey had begun. She was headed as far away from Phi-Van as she could go. She willed Phi-Van's taut and tormented face out of her mind's eye but, unaware, carried Phi-Van's story curled and growing beneath her ribs.

FOSTER MOTHER COUNTRY

Lian's first impressions of Yemen are negative. She walks out into the streets carrying the ache and grey mood of jetlag. Twenty-eight hours flying and she has landed in dust and noise and too much life, dressed in a heavy skirt and too many layers of long shirts and scarves. Sanaa is unbelievably poor-looking. Any vague romantic notions of poverty and the simple life which she might have had planted in her heart by books are peeled away. Her expectations seem as remote as her boardshorts and tanktop. And yet Sanaa, despite the unique architecture, perhaps including the unique architecture, is somehow predictable. It is a simulacrum of the stuff of coffee-table books. Sanaa is full of scurrying women hidden under black shapeless cloths. Older beggar women mingle with them, covered entirely with what look like bedspreads block-printed with red and blue and yellow. The men are tiny and wear sarongs, flip-flops and guns. She looks around, repelled. Women flow about her on the street, making an invisible line defining the space between her and them. They glance up at her briefly with black-fringed eyes. Their voices, when she catches them, are high and seemingly without consonants: frameless, boneless. The way they are dressed and the odd, faceless expressions in their eyes make her feel uncomfortable. It is as if they are animals. Her pulse rises in a helpless anger. Her chest aches and her throat is dry. Wherever she looks it is the same. A woman passes, so completely covered that she is a shapeless mound of black following behind her stiffly erect husband. Lian starts looking for the husband with two or more wives. She cannot find one, for now. There are guns everywhere. Mangy dogs skirt around her, giving ground, eyeing her, mysteriously interested in her. Green slags, fresh and wet or dried to a powder, streak the roadside. Men lounge in their shopfronts, chewing qat cross-legged exactly as they do in the photographs, ejecting streams of bright green residue metres into the footpath.

Sanaa has a heady stink, is noisy and importunate. Sanaa flows and rushes, busy with incomprehensible currents. All about her something resembling Arabic is murmured, muttered, gabbled and shrieked, the syllables jamming into one another, stretching, converging, yawning and racing away, snatched up in rapid exchanges and whisked from lips by automobiles and the flowing clothes of passers-by. Despite her four years of intensive study, she cannot understand a single word.

Photographs could never show dirt, grime, dust, damage, noise and misery like this. The bananas in a street-side cart are being dusted savagely by a man with one arm and no fingers. The dirty cloth is taped to his palm. A small boy with a birdlike frame walks past her, the side of his head rising into a swollen fistulous sore. He catches her eye and shouts something at her with a man's voice.

In photographs you look. Here you don't.

Lian's feet slowed, as if dragged through water, through mud, through honey. At the churned and bustling corner of a corroded house at the end of the *souq* she stopped, halted in the mire by a sense of intimate personal harm. The tiny hairs inside her ears stood up, prickling, sentient. She started to panic, looking around for a leering face, a stalker, a gun pointed her way. People flowed around her, staring curiously. Many eyes were on her white face and shining brown hair, on her Indian skirt and her too-red scarf. Her forearms were bare and she could feel the prickle from glances butting against them. She was exposed to the sniper glare of thousands. She could see no hostility but she was afraid. She was afraid of the small boy with his wet mouth open, whose absorbent eyes stuck to her as he passed, stumbling and bumping into people as he twisted round to look back at her.

Helena, a German girl she had met the night before through a jetlagged haze, hailed her from the human current. Helena materialised out of the crowd, unrecognisable until she made eye contact and smiled. It was a jolt. The face becoming known so near felt like a kind of blindness, enforced short-sightedness. You could pass your own mother here and not know it. She heard Phi-Van's hot whisper almost brush her ears. 'Close your mouth in public, Lian. I don't want a fish for a daughter.'

She vaguely remembered that Helena was also studying at the Language School in Sanaa University. Helena greeted her cheerily, linked arms and steered her over to some beggar women in bedspreads who were selling flat round breads the size of platters stacked high on their heads. Her panic receded.

'There is nothing in the world quite so wonderful as this bread and the women who sell it!' Helena whispered, effusive and joyous. Lian almost hated her.

Helena asked for Ghaniya in precise and military syllables, and the women chatted to her eagerly. Only their hands could be seen. The palms were stained a deep brown and orange. The cloth covering their faces was tie-dyed in large concentric circles of red, white and brown, creating the illusion of fake faces, many heads, of sacrificial eyes and colours on fish. Lian thought of the brilliant gold and purple eye she had seen on the tails of leatherjackets hauled from bright waters. She felt shut off and the first wave of homesickness rolled up and broke over her. The women gathered round in a circle, laughing and talking in clear voices but too fluidly for Lian to catch a word. She understood Helena's rejoinders, however, and could almost follow by bridging the opaque patches.

'A foreigner, yes, an *ajnabiya.*' — 'No, not Chinese. Vietnamese. From Australia.' — 'If God wills!' — 'Yes, a little.'

It was like listening to Nev on the phone.

One woman leaned towards Helena and lifted the side of her face cloth that was away from Lian. She talked quickly in this private face-to-face alcove and gave Helena two loaves. Then she dropped the cloth and turned her facelessness to Lian and greeted her formally and slowly.

'As-Salaam aleykum.'

'Waleykum as-salaam,' Lian murmured, disconcerted by the disembodied voice, startled by the syllables that had so suddenly and clearly made a phrase.

As they wandered away through the busy market Lian was about to ask Helena more about the bread women but Helena was already talking.

'I am Ghaniya's regular.'

'Do the beggar women always sell bread?'

Helena stopped still in the street and stared.

'They are NOT beggar women! What on earth made you think that?'

Lian twisted her shoulders, uncomfortable.

'I saw some begging. I assumed the bedspread signified some kind of gypsy clan. They are all old.'

'I can tell you now,' Helena said warmly, 'assumptions will shut you out in the cold here. You have to change the way you think.'

Lian blushed, angry and ashamed.

'That is traditional San'ani dress. And Ghaniya is sixteen. The black *sharshaf* and *balto* are fashions drifting in from Saudi Arabia.' Helena wrinkled her nose. Helena was also wearing a *balto*, but maroon, tailor-made from a soft acrylic fabric. It was like an ankle-length overcoat, falling from her shoulders in smooth lines to the ground.

Helena liked her Yemeni genuine and unpolluted. The partisan fervour riled Lian but she kept silent. Helena knew a lot more than she did and she was finding the easy give and take of greetings and other trade between Helena and shopkeepers, passers-by and, to her eye, completely unrecognisable women, unnerving. Helena was enjoying everything Lian was hating. As if it wasn't there to be seen as plain as rain.

'What stood out for you the most when you first walked these streets?' she asked suddenly.

Helena laughed. 'The policemen! Men in uniform with these enormous Kalashnikovs walking along holding hands with each other!'

Lian was startled.

'And the women driving cars in a *sharshaf*. That

made me long for a video camera. Now of course I wouldn't dream of wanting to film people,' Helena added quickly.

Lian's stomach lurched. Helena's assurance increased her mistrust.

She headed back to the crooked student house. The street around her was filling with men holding hands, policemen, soldiers, shopkeepers and little boys. Women careened past, invisible at the wheel of 4WDS, looking rather like daleks. Later she sat on her bed, thinking, resistant, annoyed with Helena.

She lay back, staring at the irregular white beams of the ceiling. Slowly her muscles relaxed and her anger dissipated. Why had she been so afraid? Why had she thought those coloured bundles of cloth were old? How had she known?

Europeans and Americans came to Sanaa: on business for the aid companies, for the engineering companies, for Kentucky Fried Chicken (briefly). They came for pleasure, mainly from Germany. They came as military, only from America. They came as students from universities in Denmark, Holland, England, Scotland, France, all the states of the USA, even Alaska. Europeans sought out the quaint, ancient, thick-walled houses of the old city and the Jewish and Turkish quarters, wealthy and free enough to choose bad plumbing, irregular stairs, fifth-floor kitchens and persistent cockroaches. To an outsider, to the many migratory visitors, to those with the money to restore, repair and admire, these houses were exquisite, the womb of the unique cultural experience. Many Yemenis, having grown up with the desire for clean tiles, new windows, accessible kitchens and the health and happiness granted by functional plumbing, greeted the *ajnabi* desire for insuperable domestic difficulties with incomprehension, amusement and good business sense. Predictably, those Yemenis and resident *ajnabis* who ran language schools and hotels, restored tower houses in the old city for their students to live in. Students settled, sometimes for many years, into an old-city lifestyle, the larger newer suburbs of Sanaa forming only an evanescent part of their impression of the country, forming merely the dreamlike corridor between the airport and their real Yemen; some kind of servo-studded, modernised half-way land, scattered with rusted car bodies and detritus, in which the Sheraton was to be found, glittering in Western glory, transnational. At the poolside, young Yemeni men stood serving and not looking, at least not overtly.

This was modern Sanaa, its hopes and dreams wrapped up in the new service stations and the dinged Pajeros, its suburbs stretching to the circling crown of mountains, unfurled and suckering. But its heart is still the old city, half-broken, half-spilling, half-walled in high red stone: the beak and the eye of an octopus.

Lian was to live in three different houses in Yemen, all of them either in the old city or the old quarters surrounding its wall, in that magic zone of organically grown houses winking guileless and ancient surprise at each other across crisp blue spaces. Their street doors and storerooms were rattled and obscured by noise, dust spangle, battered motorbikes and Ladas; high rooms and parapets attracted the kites that nested behind satellite dishes on the flat roofs, chicks crying in faint sounds like the pealing of distant sirens. The student house, Lian's first house, was very lovely. It was seven storeys tall, irregular, rough-hewn and impeccably restored. Sirena, the Austrian wife of a Yemeni business-man, had restored it and now managed it from the eyrie of the sixth- and seventh-floor apartments. She was a beautiful, too thin woman in her early forties, fiercely Western in dress and outlook, having survived twenty angry years in Yemen.

Lian's room was small, high, white-plastered and peaceful, supplied with a mattress, clean bedding and a desk. It also had a small tent-like wardrobe built of a light tubular frame and a plastic skin, with a zip-up door and a cardboard floor.

On the second day, she unpacked her suitcase and hung two fine silk dresses, which were crinkled from the trip to look like stormy seas. She parcelled away the clothes in the small piles in which she had bound them before leaving Adelaide, sandwiching them at the bottom of the shaky wardrobe before taking out a long blue skirt, one of Nev's shirts and a scarf with which she experimented in front of her mirror. She lay a while on her bed, staring up at the crooked beams, smiling. She went to the bathroom, fiddled with everything, cleaned the basin, then went back and stared at the ceiling, holding her hands spread at arm's length above her face, seeing the flesh of her palms translucent in the odd light. She was speaking all the while in a low, habitual murmur, renarrating to herself everything she had seen and now saw. The din from the street was audible but remote. She said a few Arabic phrases into the air, thoughtfully, as if blowing smoke rings, and then went back to the murmuring monologue that formed the thread by which she retraced herself whenever she was alone.

Her first love was her windows. Each window had an upper and lower section. The lower was made of two clear glass casements; the upper of coloured glass set in a plaster fretwork. The panes of this upper section were red and blue and yellow, divided into the segments of an ornate yet austere flower. The primary colours broke the light as it entered the room, then reformed in gentle, myriad hues on the rough white walls. The window was a compound thing. The outer panel was without glass, a geometric pattern made of plaster which cast its own, contrasting forms against the coloured glass of the flower behind it, breaking the colours there into shadows and light. The whole arrangement was in layers. *Qamariyya*, this window was called. Something that lets the moon in.

These windows were replicated wherever she looked, throughout this house and outside, with different designs and different arrangements of arabesque, floral and geometric, sometimes one, then the other as the outer fretwork.

She had almost fled from the street the night before and decided to stay in today. She read some of her Arabic grammar, then began to write to Nev and Phi-Van, Mal and Claire, Dr Qabbani and one or two uni acquaintances. The letters slowly filled with disconcerting clichés. Kaleidoscopic whirl, exotic others, the mystery of the East, the Orient, Arabia Felix. She started several anecdotes with the words 'Arabs are ...' She was passing by a world her family could not imagine but she was seeing only what they already knew and suddenly she stopped. She walked to the window and, kneeling, opened the lower casements. The sounds of the city rushed in: the clangs, roars, yelps and insect sizzle of life outside. She started in the top corner of the window among the minarets and medieval crowns of the houses and worked her way through the jigsaw view. Birds and bright washing. Glittering Sanani windows and ancient mudbrick. Seven storeys, six, five. It looked like a fantasy sweetshop, icing and ornate piping on gingerbread, each window surrounded by white relief geometric patterns, by sills and ornate lashes, each layer topped with plaster lace. The houses shimmered in the rising stench of uncombusted benzine and some other, perhaps nicer, smells she couldn't identify. Sky Channel dishes on dilapidated houses. No. A Sky Channel dish on a dilapidated house. There were nearly as many unveiled women as veiled, although all wore the *hijab*. Only a few of the men were carrying guns. Many children.

She had barely begun when she was distracted. Two men and three sheep on a motorbike passed at that moment under her window. The bike was weaving fluently around mobs of careless children and piles of refuse. The sheep were stacked one upon the other wedged in between the two skinny men. The guy at the back trailed a grimy chequered and tasselled head-cloth, a *mshadda*, up to his chin in sheep. He leaned back against the spindly props of his arms. The guy at the front leaned forward over the handlebars. The three sheep were a mass of piled hair and flesh. Two had their heads one way, the middle one faced out alone the other. Their legs stuck out like marionettes' limbs, held up and then floppy from the joints. Their faces had expressions of apathy or resignation, giving the ensemble a foolish gaiety.

She had stopped feeling jetlagged or even timid. She clattered down the stairs in search of Helena.

Out on the street, the hot dust spurted behind motorbikes and swirled upward into the spangled air. Children ran back and forth playing with bits of rubbish. Ragged shreds and shards of plastic floated onto the tidal flats of the streetsides. Stone walls rose above heavy blue doors which had what almost resembled Bronze Age axes for knockers. Some plastered walls were ornamented with raised plaster snakes or four-legged animals. One had an aeroplane in plaster relief above the door. Another a machine gun. Several had the words *Ma sha Allah*, an exclamation affirming beauty indirectly by mentioning only God's will. Dogs lay sleeping in the receding shade rims under the cobbled walls. A small girl in a peaked hood was drawing in the dust with a brown feather. Her sure line fanned out to her feet, returned, ducked in and made a bird.

Lian watched and felt herself flying, something beating at her heart to get in. She walked on quickly before her presence could shake the stillness of the dust bird and its maker.

Boys were playing soccer in a dry rubbish-filled creek-bed that ran through the city, catching the ball between their feet in their long shirts.

Kites wheeled in the sky.

A cat tried to eat a KitKat wrapper.

Helena took Lian shopping for clothes. Helena's motherliness towards her shook her, and shopping made her feel exposed — to the crowd, to the shop-keepers, to Helena.

Women's clothes shops on Sharia Jamal were of several kinds. There were the wild, floating colour arcades of chiffon and silk, usually off the roll but with some dresses ready-made, and the strange softly fluttering hollows of blackness that sold the *sharashif*, the *balto*, the *litham* and black *maqrama*: all the black outer garments behind which women lived in public, unknown. Helena was at ease and even delighted in these shops. Perhaps she was acting a little, to make a point. But, bit by bit. Lian's interest was caught. The black embroidery on black was very fine. The styles, so apparently uniform at first, began to differentiate themselves and she became conscious of preferences: a puffed sleeve, not bunched at the shoulder. Ribbon (black satin) and scroll embroidery, no faux jet ornament. They entered cave after cave of exquisite black finery, Helena bargaining and dressing Lian up. Shopkeepers were amused, enjoying the theatre the two *ajnabiyas* presented, praising them repeatedly for adopting Yemeni dress.

To disappear from sight. To dive and sink in the crowd. To be free. Suddenly Lian saw it: not Helena's gesture of cultural respect, but the freedom given by deflecting all eyes. She bought suddenly, speaking shy Arabic for the first time that day: a black *balto* (very large, the shopkeeper said, looking up at her, worriedly) and a blue *hijab*. Face uncovered, with *hijab* not *maqrama*, she would be clearly an educated, university young woman, the shopkeeper said. 'This is the way of many of the university girls.'

When she stepped out of the shop beside Helena, the street around her had changed. She was no longer

49

some impediment in the flow of passers-by. The eyes, even when they did seek out her face, turned away again quickly, seemingly respectfully. The girls and women stood out much more clearly to her, as if she had taken some drug that made them visible. Their eyes, brown, black, large, almond shaped, fine lashed or small and smiling, caught her often, just for a moment, an observation, a thought, and then were gone. The occasional university girl in *hijab* occasionally smiled, an inward and fleeting smile, but Lian thought it might have been for her. And some were so graceful, under fine cut *balto* and fluttering *maqrama* wings. They looked like black angels from behind. Some were dirty and poor: wearing fashions Lian had not seen in the shops. And some were dusty and not poor, dust riding up a carelessly worn *balto*. Lian's heart lifted and she walked in easy pleasure beside Helena, grateful and contrite.

Lian settled into Sanaa, willing it to be home. Classes started on the third day and her life was instantly very full. The words, becalmed between four walls, tamed by the teacher, began to announce themselves again, present themselves to her for recognition.

In Arabic Prose in the early mornings, the class began reading a story from the *Kitab Alf Layla wa-Layla*, a diffuse four-volume compendium of stories which Lian only recognised weeks later to be the *Arabian Nights*. The story was a slow and elaborate travelogue of a journey under the sea. She struggled with it. It was intricate, peppered with many new nouns and difficult concepts. The language was old, repetitious and ornate, having almost no momentum. The first frustration was the fact that every character was named Abdallah. Abdallah the Merman, Abdallah the Baker, Abdallah the King, Abdallah the Fisherman. For the first two weeks of readings she was lost in a sea of Abdallahs, never quite sure among all the unfamiliar words and phrases which character was being referred to. It seeped into her dreams.

Everyone was Abdallah. They looked the same and performed the same gestures and said the same phrases. Understanding the words only blended them, made them more uniform. She started to think that the story provided a similarly colourful monotony and stasis as the world around; and she started to think as the early scholars had: this culture is ageless, changeless, uniform.

Abdallah the Fisherman stood at the shore as he had every day of his life, winding his net in loops ready to wade out and cast it into the reflective shallows. His heart was heavy. His wife lay on the straw, having given birth to his tenth child. The sea had been empty for days and in that time the family had not eaten properly. He was blessed with children but afraid that today they would not eat at all. He prayed and cast.

All day he cast and the sea stared back, calm
and empty. At nightfall he had nothing and headed
home, the hunger of his wife and nine children
sitting in his belly. One more day and her milk
would dwindle and tiny Abdallah would most
certainly die.

It was only a story, not even a particularly riveting story. They read no more than a page each Wednesday, for there were many other exercises. Grammar, poetry, Koran, contemporary Yemeni dialect, conversation. The story, however, was a sea story. Helena and the two other advanced students hated it, for it was slow-moving and, no sooner had it rushed towards a conclusion of a kind, than the tide turned and its finalities ebbed away to return in a different form another day. It would not cohere in Lian's mind as a story. Some fundamental disconnection from the language made the syntax of the narrative incoherent, and she could sense that this came from her. It was almost like a physical barrier, a blindness, deafness, dumbness. She could see the story dimly through odd phrases that leapt out at her and stuck, but the sentences would not come together to form a paragraph. The woman in the straw, and the empty almost solid sea were sketched in block colour in her mind. These images had to carry all meanings, for nothing else would hang together enough to be memorable. Abdallah himself was invisible and unimaginable.

She had, in all her Arabic studies, read much simpler

stories. Her self-esteem dissolved in a day. She had been given preprepared stories. Arabic in its natural habitat was a wild and slippery thing, a very different creature from the domesticated, even crippled Arabic she had learned in Australia.

Lian wandered past the donkey market in the old city, feeling uncomfortable in the strange clothes, hoping she wouldn't run into any Europeans who knew her.

Sirena had looked at her aghast.

'Have you gone Muslim on us now?' Her voice rose slightly at the end and Lian thought of Phi-Van. She felt drained.

'This doesn't mean I am Muslim. Christian women all over the Middle East cover their hair.' Her words felt hollow. Somehow Sirena's disgust was stronger than knowledge.

But, having adopted *hijab* and *balto*, she could not discard them. She watched the Yemenis watch other European women, shout to them, and she could not put herself back in the line of fire.

'I love you!'

'USA!'

'Thank you!'

'Please!'

'Hi honey, I'm home!'

'Chinese! Chinese!'

It all ceased when the silence of what she imagined was anonymity descended on her. In that peace she suddenly felt more at ease and more as if she belonged. Helena laughed when she tried to describe this.

'Oh yes, I felt the same. But you know, Lian, you will never fit in here. None of us will. It is an illusion. The trick is to enjoy the privilege of being an outsider who knows her way round. There is no way any of us would really become Yemeniyas, Christian ones or otherwise.'

'What about the Russians?'

'They marry Muslims and live here,' Helena said simply.

Four young children rushed up to her staring into her face, holding onto her *balto* with grimy hands, breathless with excitement.

'Pen! Pen! Pen! Paper!?' they cried out in Arabic.

She looked at them in confusion, unsure if that was really what she had heard.

'Pen! Pen? Pen? Paper?' A note of pleading crept into their voices.

She began to rummage in her bag for paper. Suddenly she was the centre of a squabbling storm of children, crying and jostling like seagulls. A man in a grimy *mshadda* waded through them roughly, silencing them with a cry of '*Aib!* Shame!' They stood back, eyeing him, eyeing Lian, waiting. He said something to

Lian, unsmiling. She thought he probably told her to leave. She apologised softly and walked away as the street melted back into its usual form behind her. The cluster of children disappeared back into the interstices or hollows of the buildings. She hid her face in her *hijab* and ploughed, head down, into the crowds.

After a while she felt a shift within her, a slipping of sands at a tide line. She felt that walking outside dressed the way the Europeans and Americans did, blithely, blindly, would have been like walking down the city mall in Adelaide with bare breasts.

'Hi honey, I'm home' seemed mild under the circumstances and she found herself liking Yemeni men for their restraint as she listened to others decry them for their disrespect.

Then, after a while, that explanation became brittle with overuse and Lian became angry again.

As the fisherman made his way home, praying to God to sustain his wife and children, the rich aroma of fresh baked bread assailed him and he felt dizzy with hunger. Times were hard and a crowd was gathered for the last bake at Abdallah the Baker's stall. Abdallah the Fisherman hovered for a moment at the back of the clamouring crowd. The people were shouting with urgency and irritation, waving coins and other produce in the air over their neighbours' heads. Abdallah the Fisherman had nothing to wave. He turned to go

*but the Baker had seen the hunger and despair in
the Fisherman's eyes and called him up to the stall.
He pressed eleven loaves and some coins into the
Fisherman's hands, saying, 'Take these to your
wife and children, and get her a little meat as well.'*

*Abdallah the Fisherman went crimson with
shame. 'I have nothing to give you except for this
net.' He started to ease the net off his shoulder but
the Baker stopped him.*

*'What sort of man would I be if I took your
livelihood? You can pay me back tomorrow with
some of your catch.'*

*Abdallah the Fisherman's wife cried with relief
and called blessings down upon the Baker's head.*

*But the next day the sea was as empty as a
night sky. The surface stared back at Abdallah,
rippling softly, cruel and impenetrable, withholding
all life. Abdallah the Fisherman made his way
back past the Baker and told him of his unlucky
day, shamefaced. The Baker again pressed
eleven loaves and some coins upon him, saying
that times would change and that the
Fisherman could pay him back with fish from
his catch.*

In grammar they read the Koran. She faxed Nev and Phi-
Van on the back of a case-ending exercise done using
the *Surat al-Rahman*. The fax traffic control operator sat
in his high booth, directing words around the world.

He looked at the back of the paper as it fed through the machine.

'You study Koran? Are you Muslim?'

Lian's hair rose under her *hijab*. What would he think with her fax scrawled on the back of holy verses? She blushed. How could she have been so stupid?

'Our teacher teaches us grammar using the most perfect form of the language. No, not yet.'

He looked pleased. He gave it back to her.

'*Inshallah,*' he said.

'Muslim yet?' he asked every time she came in to send a fax.

'Not yet.'

Traffic control, high in his booth with technology, wished her godspeed.

I am feeling pretty strange, she wrote to Nev. *The good thing is nobody notices my eccentricities because they are expected of me.*

Don't get too lonely. Make some friends. Go out to dinner every night with people, promise me you will, but stay away from the men, Phi-Van wrote back.

For forty days Abdallah the Baker kept death from the Fisherman's family. The sea gave nothing, even though Abdallah the Fisherman worked all day in a frenzy, the shame of his debt to the Baker intensifying with each passing day. His wife said that he needed to trust that God, who had given

*them the Baker's generosity, would deliver them
from their straitened circumstances. But words
could no longer lift the despondency that settled
upon the Fisherman.*

*On the forty-first day he found himself
questioning the existence of God.*

*'Lord, if today I cannot pay the Baker, I would
be better off casting myself into the sea, for it has
as good as taken my life and my honour.'*

*He cast his net, praying gloomily that the sea
give him life, not death. The net felt heavy but not
with the quivering weight of living fish. He hauled
with all his might and eventually landed a pile of
mean and grimy rubbish. He cast again, praying,
despair settling upon him. Again the net was
heavy, a different weight this time. His raw palms
strained against the lines and eventually he landed
the huge load. It was the awkward, sodden bulk of
a rotting dead donkey. He looked at its pallid eye
sockets. Then he was forced to move further along
the shore, for the donkey reeked.*

A young girl of about twelve, with a face both sweet and
cunning, raced up to Lian and grabbed her by the hand,
staring up at her lovingly with black laughing eyes, and
twining her arms like creepers around Lian's. Pleading
and cajoling, she dragged Lian towards the courtyard
of her house. Outside the courtyard, three donkeys
munched on straw, ignoring the visitor. Yasmin begged

for a picture and Lian took several. In each picture there was one more brother or sister lined up with Yasmin against the sunlit wall. The donkeys ignored the excitement, sour-faced.

The following week Lian went by the donkey market with copies of the photos for Yasmin. The children clamoured in excitement around her, staring at the pictures as if they were food and drink. Then the pictures vanished and Yasmin thanked her politely, suddenly restrained in her manner. There was a slight lull and Lian, satisfied that she had at least followed the main threads of the interaction, made a move to leave. Yasmin was suddenly shot through with excitement again. She hung on Lian's arm, begging her to visit, just for a few minutes. Lian gave her a dollar coin with kangaroos on it but Yasmin's efforts increased to a frantic pleading. Lian gave in and Yasmin, smiling and swelling with pride, glanced from side to side to see who was watching her as she led an *ajnabiya* into her house.

The house tunnelled upward in a seemingly random fashion. The stairway opened up here and there into rooms and courtyards, all dusty and sadly lit through chinks and fallen ceilings. At a turning of the uneven stair, a woman stood washing in an unlit alcove, her head uncovered and arms bare. She turned and cast an appraising look over Lian, then turned away after muttering the obligatory response to Lian's shy greeting. At another landing Yasmin suddenly disappeared and Lian was left hovering at a darkened turn in a strange house. She could hear and feel that there were people all around her: layers of women, above and below and to the sides. A woman suddenly appeared next to her, having descended a hidden stairway. She had a sweet face, too, but looked Lian up and down without smiling. She held the dollar coin.

'What is this worth?' she asked.

'Nothing,' Lian said, obscurely ashamed.

The woman invited Lian to follow her. She ushered her through a door to an alcove in which Lian removed her shoes, then through another door into a crowded and well-furnished room, probably the only furnished room in the labyrinth. Yasmin rushed up to her, breathless. There were more than ten women of all different ages seated in the *mafraj*, smoking from a single *madaa* with a very long purple pipe and mouthpiece. The sweet smell of moist crushed tobacco filled the room. The air was thick, smelling of something deeper, too, something physical. Three women crowded around Lian, greeting and introducing themselves. Lian missed the names and relationships. They tried to take her *balto* from her and, although everyone was dressed in coloured and varied dresses and most had their heads uncovered, Lian was suddenly reserved. She sensed an urgent desire in the room to check her out: to see what sort of clothes she wore, what sort of body she had. Then, having refused to undress with them, Lian was unsure of herself. Had she insulted them? Had she broken some law of hospitality? She blushed as she was led, swathed in her cloak, across the room to the far end. Yasmin pointed down to two babies sleeping on the cushions, her young face softening for the first time to something quieter and sweeter than the doublespeak of her fine features and childish malice.

'My sister gave birth to a son one week ago,' she said softly, gesturing to a pale young woman propped in the cushions to one side.

Hoping she had understood correctly, Lian stuttered, 'Congratulations. *Mabruk.*' She looked at the babies and murmured, '*Mashallah,*' in conventional admiration. The young woman stared at her with large black eyes and didn't answer.

'He died,' Yasmin said into her ear.

'Oh.' Lian jumped a little, as if stung by the word, unsure. Could *maat* be more than a word? She looked down, bewildered, at the tiny forms curled on the cushions at her feet. The baby nearest her was curled around himself, his face glowing, the faint down on his head shining blue in the light from the window. The other had one arm stretched above her head, her eyelashes small dark crescents on her cheeks, a deep red mouth open. Each had one ear showing, curled and translucent as a shell.

The young woman in the corner turned to the wall and Lian recognised in the gesture what she could not comprehend in the room and the faces around. Neither of these babies was hers. She felt as though she were wading in water, unable to run, slow: too slow.

'I am sorry,' Lian wanted to say but her voice had left her. Yasmin led her to a gap on the cushions.

Everyone looked at her and a silence fell on the room.

An old woman with fierce eyes, who was drawing deeply from the *madaa*, looked up straight at Lian and exhaled. Smoke parted in a rising, curlicued moustache, framing the leathery face.

'Where are you from?'

'Australia, in the south.'

'Are you married?'

'No.'

'How old are you?'

'Twenty-three.'

The old woman turned away and began chatting to her neighbour. Immediately the women on either side of Lian began talking to her, their eyes eager, their hands feeling for hers and rubbing at her calluses and rough cuticles, touching her. Lian tolerated it, trying to be correct, be polite, but her sense of self-respect was draining from her. She felt squeezed, packaged, humiliated. She also felt an instant liking for Ammat al-Alim to her left and an equally strong dislike for Ammat al-Karim to her right. Ammat al-Alim had a reserved manner and an unintrusive eye. The fine curve of her body over her raised knee, the quiet, even respectful diffidence, washed over Lian and strengthened her. Ammat al-Karim's manner was soft and excessively refined, but her eyes slid over Lian's face and breast like oil.

'No children?' she asked in a soft, sly voice, smiling.

'No. As I said, I am unmarried.' Lian suddenly wondered, with slight shock, whether she was being insulted but was still too bewildered with piecing together the phrases coming her way to be able to piece together the strange currents in the room.

'*Inshallah*, soon.' Ammat al-Alim murmured, her voice conventional, even bored, but without malice. Unfamiliar as everything was, Lian sensed a reprimand to Ammat al-Karim in the careful re-establishment of conventional niceties.

'*Inshallah.*'

Yasmin scampered in and out of the room, the only child present other than the sleeping babies. Lian explained in halting Arabic how she had befriended Yasmin and returned with the photos. Ammat al-Karim asked Yasmin something about the photos. Yasmin shook her head, said something looking sideways at Lian, her fine lip curling. Lian reconstructed the last words of the hot whisper:

'... above a *donkey*!'

Lian sat with sweat pricking from her skin under her clothes. She knew she was blushing. The feeling of having given insult was unbearable and increased a strange mixture of dislocation, distress and anger at being trapped in this room, at the mercy of whatever it was that was happening, compelled to feel that she should know and do the right thing. She was stung at having made such a mistake, and stung too because she had liked the donkeys, liked their nonchalant disregard for the jostling children lined on the ledge above them. She had thought the photos particularly good.

She could almost see the torn fragments drifting in a straw-covered room from the worn fingers of the woman with the dollar coin, the laughing girl and the donkeys parted.

Yasmin was suddenly standing in front of her, laughing. She had something in her hands. She could hear the older women laughing loudly across the room. Their mouths were open, their eyes unfriendly but eager. Yasmin, watching all the women around, said something rapidly, breathlessly and the laughter increased. Ammat al-Karim leaned up to Yasmin and whispered in her ear, giggling. Ammat al-Alim shook her head slightly at Yasmin, unsmiling. Lian looked across the long *mafraj* to the childless mother. Her glance was met with an unsmiling, black look, a momentary glance of excoriated despair. The look froze her. She sat, her body taking as little space as possible, her *balto* wrapped around her knees and tucked underneath her.

Yasmin shrugged cheekily, looked away from Ammat al-Alim, and sat down. She turned upon Lian, wriggling closer, leaned in and half opened her hand. She had a wad of cottonwool. With suddenly serious eyes focused on Lian's face, she moved the wad an inch away from Lian's chest, belly and lightly between her legs, without touching her. The room hushed. Lian stiffened but didn't know what to do. She could feel

Yasmin's heartbeat leaping against her arm. After a few seconds Lian couldn't stand it and raised her own hand in a deflecting movement. Yasmin stopped, grinned at her, and slowly opened the cotton wool. At the centre it was soaked in blood. Yasmin laughed in her face and ran out the door. The women around rocked with laughter, with the exception of Ammat al-Alim and the bereaved mother. Ammat al-Alim got up and walked out and Lian didn't see her again.

Lian stood up. She wanted to run and cry. She took leave clumsily, thanking them, and stumbled down the stairs and away from the house. The old woman on the diwan opposite had glanced at her once. Lian saw disgust.

After a few steps, Lian was angry with herself, with them, with Yemen. The image of the room and herself in it preyed on her. The image of herself stung most of all. Gawky and awkward, apologetic without knowing what for. The pain and the laughter in the room ate away at her. She pulled out the dictionary and put together the phrase: *It is not hospitable, not cultured, to laugh upon a stranger, a guest in your house.*

Despite walking through the donkey market so armed, however, Lian did not find Yasmin again.

Lian was losing her strength and knew it. Where she had been silent, she had become voluble. Where she had been solitary, she now sought out company, even of

Helena, whom she found annoying. Where she had known her own mind, remained aloof, even arrogant, she now felt bewildered, torn and often ashamed for no reason. For a little while she blamed the *hijab*. Astounded at how eroded she felt herself to be, she wondered if costume could count for so much. But at night, when she thought it through, everything she was feeling had nothing new or fresh about it. It was as familiar as a stale smell shut away in a long disused trunk of discarded clothes. It was herself that she could smell, the self long boarded up, bound in hoop iron, long stowed. The self none of her techniques of deflection could protect here. It was not herself that was vulnerable but her means of protecting and ignoring it. No-one was here who had known her before. Nothing had a history with her in it.

She found herself standing naked, malnourished, ugly and, worst of all, weak and needy, out there in every encounter for all to see if they cared to look.

A blonde woman was striding up the street, taller and more visible than any man. Her hair fluttered in the breeze. Lian felt the crowd around her turn and stare, eddying and reforming. Lian stared too. The woman was proud and angry. Her shoulders were stiff and her steps assertive. She didn't respond to the *Hellos* and *How are yous* and *Welcomes* and *I love yous* offered to get her attention, although it was clear that her attention was bristling. She walked in a straight line up the street. Coming towards her was a small family, a black-covered woman holding the hands of three brightly dressed small children. They stretched as a fragile net across the walkway. The crowd parted to let them through, some people stepping onto the road, others easing past. The blonde woman walked straight through them without looking back. Her jeans parted the hands as if they were not there. The Yemeni woman stopped and stared after her and Lian caught her eyes, startled and questioning, brightening to anger from their peephole in the black *litham*. Lian was acutely aware of being foreign too. The eyes were still asking something of her personally and, involuntarily, Lian raised her hands palm upwards and mouthed an apology. The eyes softened and the family turned, reformed and walked away.

It had all happened in a split second but it was a conversation.

He made his third cast and again the net was heavy. He could not hope but he prayed quietly. His blood stained the grey rope. With one last pull he wrenched the net and its load into the shallows and onto the sand. It contained one giant fish, moving languidly.

'As-Salaam aleykum,' the fish said to him in a soft voice.

'Waleykum as-salaam!' Abdallah answered automatically, staring at his catch, astonished.

He made out the form of a greenish human
being through the net. The fish had the head
and torso of a man and the long tail of a fish.
Abdallah's heart began to race and he quickly
pegged the net down.

The wall in the vacant lot beyond the garden of her house was graffitied with strange slogans, daubed in heavy, childish Arabic with brush and various colours. Summon the stars. Summon the falcons. The stars are the highest. Lian transcribed the alien, cryptic self-assertion into her book, looked it up in the dictionary but could not solve it. Later, when the Stars and the Falcons, and the Peace seemed to appear everywhere, particularly in the high voices of young boys, she gradually realised that the word for summon and the word for soccer team were almost the same.

Between two gnarled peppercorn trees, wedged up against a mudbrick wall on 26 September Street, a prematurely wrinkled and smiling man cooked large aluminium trays of *bizr*, fried pumpkin and melon seeds. His shop was defined by hessian and woven plastic wheatbags nailed between the trunks of the trees and by its contents: sacks of grain formed a bag wall to the street and old sacks formed his perch back against a trunk. He chewed qat all day and sold the aromatic roasted kernels to passing cars and pedestrians. He had a long fluoro bar strung between the trees, illuminating his stand at night when he also watched television. The

Stars, the Falcons and the Peace. Lian couldn't work out how he obtained power for his little set and light and was too shy to ask him.

On the street the young men swaggered, gathered and conversed. A young man stooped to tie a passing boy's shoelaces. Men picked lint off younger men's shoulders and listened to tapes of Fuad al-Kipsi and Fairuz at street-side stalls. At the *aseer* shop at the end of Shari'a Jamal, men and boys hovered in a fug of ripe mango and pressed orange. The pavement was sticky.

The street was exciting, perfumed with cheap frankincense and littered with trays of trashy toys. Flocks of covered girls floated in and out of perfumeries, trinket shops and, for the wealthy and the dreamers, glittering mirrored gold shops. The long street fluttered with trails of multicoloured chiffons and floral rayons, diaphanous flags hanging off the roll in front of draperies. The street suggested the colour, perfume, gorgeous glory of women: by implication, by a small step of the imagination, these fabrics could be seen in the mind's eye clothing a living form.

The brightly coloured, noisy display of men on the street was far more overt, men like cockerels, men ardently preening, adjusting their shirts, stopping to straighten little boys' shirts, perfumed; men were visible, fishing with their colour and vivacity for attention. Men were so remote. Lian almost wished she could cruise the street arm in arm with Phi-Van, watching the beautiful boys.

He could show this wonder of the sea, charge
a small fee to crowds, feed his family, make his
fortune. A sweet, nervous happiness crept into
his bones and he felt lightheaded. But the fish
was talking to him and he started to pay attention.

'Release me, O Fisherman, and God will
reward your mercy.'

'Who are you, O Fish?'

'I am of the people of the sea. I am one of
the sons of Adam, like yourself, and a Muslim,
like yourself. Submission to the will of God
prevented me from tearing your net apart and
swimming free.'

The happiness drained out of Abdallah the
Fisherman. His only catch in forty-one days and
it was a Muslim, a man, albeit a strange one, cast
upon his mercy. He was silent.

'Release me and we can become brothers. I will
meet you here every day and exchange the fruits of
the sea for the fruits of the land.'

Abdallah the Fisherman listened dreamily to
the Merman describing the rubies, sapphires and
topaz stones from under the sea. He agreed to
release the Merman.

'My name is Abdallah of the Sea. Let us recite
the Fatiha together and we will truly be brothers.'

They recited the Fatiha. The Merman had a
strange accent but a beautiful voice. Abdallah the
Fisherman loosened the cord of the net.

Abdallah of the Sea leapt into the waves and disappeared, looking much like any large fish or dolphin. Abdallah of the Land stared out at the empty sea, blue and shining to the horizon, reprimanding himself bitterly for having thrown away his only chance to feed his family. But just as despair had settled into his heart, Abdallah the Merman reappeared in the shallows, carrying a basket woven of seagrasses. The Merman handed the basket to the Fisherman, and each promised to meet the other on the following day. Abdallah the Fisherman looked into the basket and cried out to the Glory of God. It was filled with rubies like eggs and sapphires the size of which confounded his reason. A great weight lifted from his shoulders and with a light step he made his way straight to Abdallah the Baker and told him everything that had transpired. Then he forced half the basketload on the Baker, saying, 'Half of my catch!'

The Baker closed his shop and went home with the Fisherman. The large family rejoiced that night, celebrating with a feast put on by Abdallah the Baker.

FOSTER MOTHER TONGUE

In Arabic some things are said or written twice, the second word there to ensure that the right choice of meaning is made for the first and vice versa. A man is just and fair-minded, a woman brave and courageous, a judge has intuition, insight, discernment in the ways of men. Each word could be many things but together they build a concept, an assurance as to meaning here and now, in this moment on the page. They are stones and it takes more than one to make a building or a wall or a well. Sometimes, for added security and for rhythm, even for architectural symmetry and grace, four words meaning the same thing are used. There can be no doubt as to meaning but this goes beyond establishing simple certainties. This emphasises the qualities of the subject, this carries them into a proclamation of meaning, ornamented and important. Characters with these four-corner attributes can only change in the course of a story under considerable pressure. Four corners of certainty and the stakes are higher.

But writing Arabic seemed to be attempting to sculpt with water. The language ran through Lian's fingers and was gone before she could make a phrase of her own. She was driven to learn the simple, tried and proven phrases of daily intercourse and forget for the time being any attempt to drink and breathe Arabic.

Lian, Helena and two other students were packed in the back of a large Landcruiser, nicknamed a Monica Lewinsky, heading out to a village called al-Hajara for a picnic. Lian had burnt her hand making coffee that morning. Water boiled reluctantly at the altitude of the Sanaa plateau but boiled quiet and hot, and the full pot had spilt over her left hand. It was bandaged, bound into a single stiff paw. Lian nursed it in her lap, the day's outing marred by the throbbing pulse under the stinging skin.

Their driver, Hassan, ignored them and danced privately to the piping voice of Fuad al-Kipsi, which wound like thin threads on a wind from the stereo. The 4WD in front, the older, beamier Layla al-Alawi, stopped suddenly in a raucous street market of one of a succession of dusty stony villages and the Monica pulled up behind. Both drivers got out and disappeared. The passengers shuffled, and looked around.

'Qat,' said Helena, noticing Lian's curious and unsettled expression.

The village was made of stone from the surrounding plains, cliffs and escarpments. It was built of brown and black boulders, volcanic, a vaguely ordered mound in the bleak plain. The goats and sheep were thin but not as thin as the black and gold dogs that slipped in and out between rubble walls and tin. People shouted over watermelons and bananas and apricots the size of marbles but most were shouting over the bunches of qat, which, apart from the green mottled melons, were the only green thing as far as the eye could see. The village gave the impression that the huts from which it was made were lower than head height: they were squat rubble mounds with doors like black mouths. Women and children stared at the two 4WDS without warmth.

Lian looked away. This was ordinary life here and she felt obscurely ashamed to be observing it. The two vehicles and their exotic occupants were perhaps being sized up. What could this village want that it could gain by kidnapping them? Everything. The Monica and the Layla, for a start. Embarrass the government by capturing Swiss, Australian and German nationals and ask for clean water, a school and hospital, a road for trade, and some younger donkeys.

Suddenly there was a shrieking and yelping immediately behind the Monica. A young man was kicking a dog, repeatedly, brutally. Ana and Helena cried out. Lian, without thinking, shouted in a strange, reverberating voice, 'Shame on you!' and the car shook with their gestures. The man stopped instantly, shocked into stillness. It was the first time she had spoken Arabic without thought. Her heart was beating but settling as the others laughed and praised her. They waited, talking about Yemenis and dogs, about their own dogs at home. Each of them had a beloved dog, each different.

Another man in a soiled white *futa* and red *mshadda* appeared at the side of the Monica, holding three small, plump puppies. They were fat and perfect and ordinary, and Lian relaxed. Helena and Ana leaned over to the side with her and the man must have heard them murmur their appreciation, for he looked up and smiled. He held up one of the puppies in a weathered but gentle hand, and they shook their heads, thinking he wanted to give it to them. He put it down with the other two in the dust and strode away. They stared down and a vague disquiet rose in Lian. What if one staggered under the Monica? Into the road?

The man suddenly returned with a fourth puppy in his hand. He squatted down without looking up and suddenly a long curved knife with a thin blade appeared in his hand. Ana and Helena screamed and slammed the window with their palms. He didn't look up until the last minute and then he glanced up, unsmiling, the long blade against the blind beast's throat.

75

The scene was suddenly dreamy. Something heavy and black settled into Lian and she sat immobile, looking, but from a great distance. But Ana was out of the car and challenging him, screaming abuse at him in Arabic and German, telling him off for playing games, ordering him about with all the authority of his grandmother, her slight eighteen-year-old frame quivering with rage. He put down the knife and grinned at her, and, with her help, carried all the puppies back inside the fence of a house yard. Ana was gone a long time, but they could hear her voice over the fence. Helena and the other student chatted, laughing through their relief, admiring Ana's guts. Lian smiled but felt nothing. She was bleak and hollow. She could see over and over the bright drops of blood on the knife and the tiny wriggle of life leaving, as if the next second in the story had really happened. She had done nothing. A despair about everything it meant for her to be here (and she was not sure what any of it meant) had rooted her to the spot. The cruel theatre had been for her benefit, to ask *her* what it all meant: how far she, a stranger, would go to protect a dog. She was glad of Ana, impressed and relieved, but she herself had been unable to react, and, even if the others didn't know, in one sense his point was proven. She stared down at her swathed and useless hand and felt like screaming.

Ana returned, elated and cheery. He was playing a joke. He had several dogs and, unusual for a Yemeni, thought quite highly of them and took some care of them. He showed them all to her, was a kindly and intelligent man. He had loved having her intervene and thought well of all the *ajnabiyat* for it. He would not have really killed it.

Lian said nothing. She felt she loved Ana then, for her innocence and for her immediate, thoughtless *stepping over*. She thought, with strange, slow clarity from the centre of the blackness and dizziness in which she still sat, that he would certainly have killed it to make his point; for what is a puppy, here? And if she, the real target, had been able to react, as she longed to have done? This sat at the heart of her despair. How could she have sat still? And how right could it have been to value a dog so passionately, here?

The Merman gave him daily gifts of the fruits of the sea: pearls and rubies and emeralds the size of green pears. In return he gave the Merman fruits of the land: apples, oranges, lemons and Tihama grapes that looked like round red pearls.

They still met at the seashore and chatted about religion, politics, and the nature of sameness and difference.

A shadow story was nosing out Lian's tracks. She was on the other side of the world but her mother's tight, yearning face was at her heels every night. It howled, out alone on mountaintops, a lonely moon voice. She couldn't bear it. Not because it wrung her heart; not much could. Phi-Van's journey was a larger and more pressing fact, a greater story. It pressed against her chest at night and muffled her throat.

Phi-Van's story was insatiable and needed generations to assuage it.

Reading Arabic broke the bounds of Lian's imaginary world. This was one of its enticements. Picking through the words and phrases for sense and to visualise the imaginary world of the text was so painstaking that her usual paths fragmented, broke and dissipated, replaced by something entirely new. Lian's reading usually took her to the same spaces: the same beach, the same field, the same house, regardless of the characters, the dramas or the period: these were provided by props and costumes, infinitely movable and renewable furnishings. Her bookworld was a strange, rather bare space, familiar to her from earliest childhood. It had a wooden floor, could have storeys added, and had the feel of an expressionist theatre. If a staircase was required, no matter how ornate, what she would get would be a bare simulacrum of a stair. A second storey would be a suggestive makeshift mezzanine. Lighting was often darker than in the story she was reading. This house was always near the sea, to accommodate her love of sea stories, and no matter how far-flung the action of a tale, it was simulated within reach of the house rather than taking her away.

This house had seemed infinite. It was festooned with the costumes of past readings and could fit itself to anything.

Reading was like playing in a cupboard. One could imagine anything, had to imagine everything.

Arabic broke it to pieces and, by the time she reached Yemen, Lian's imagination had also settled on a strange shore, with a strange, misty horizon and under strange seas. Everything was murky and was elsewhere. Unable to cohere, even coalesce, the house vanished. It was as if she had reached the limits of imagination but could also not return.

University had freed Lian from the Island. Her life returned to its refrain in the holidays but moved inexorably on in the stanzas. And each time she returned to the Island it was the same but she had changed.

At eighteen she had lost interest in everything except Arabic language studies. She floated around campus in a daze, only coming to life in the language sessions. Her teacher was a gentle, formal woman in her fifties who answered any questions on women in the Middle East with noncommittal, polite phrases which had a measure of exhaustion to them. Dr Suhayr Qabbani handed over the strange words and phrases in small daily packages, bundles of beauty and mystery. Lian's love for them had its roots in the formalities of these gestures. Arabic carries the word of God direct to the heart and then back, Dr Qabbani told her. She scraped through everything else but by third year was reading laboriously in Arabic and was top of her class.

But the words were as discrete as pebbles collected on a beach. She tried to read words, not sentences. Before she even read words she read letters. *Jiim* was beautiful, especially in isolation. The eye of a fish and the long, curled tail. *Ha* was his eyeless sister and *Kha* was *Jiim* in death. *Alif* was tall and elegant, the symbol of unisex grace. *Miim* lay like a pebble on the floor of sentences, shining and wet.

Sun letters melted together, the hot consonants dissolving *Lam*, the definite article; moon letters stood out, sharp and cool, each consonant ringing clear.

Arabic severed her from her friends and family in minute but insurmountable ways. It was as estranging as the sea was silencing. She yearned to study in an Arab country. She studied and did nothing else.

'What are you studying at uni, Lian?'

'Arabic.'

'Oh. That's a very strange thing to be interested in. Why Arabic?'

At first, each time the question was asked, she tried to justify the language for its relevance to European history, its literature, its beauty, its necessity to cultural reconciliation, but gradually she became tongue-tied. Infinite variations of the theme *They are Moslems, aren't they? Mohammedans. Terrorists? Why would you, a woman, study them? They abuse their women, don't they?* would muffle every attempt.

She was also a failure in the eyes of Nev and Phi-Van, Mal and Claire, and her cousins.

'Why not Vietnamese?' Phi-Van was bitter and disappointed.

'Because.' Lian was calm. 'I'm not Vietnamese. I'm Australian.'

'You're not Arab,' Phi-Van said quietly, very angry.

'At least that is absolutely clear to everybody.'

Lian could never be Vietnamese. She had shut her ears and soul to any knowledge of Vietnam which her mother might reflect, knowledge which, in any case, Phi-Van held close and tight. The slope kids at school made Lian's outsider status painfully clear. Australian kids called her a slope but the Vietnamese should know.

'What have that Allah lot got to do with us?' Nev asked.

'Nothing!' Lian said, exasperated.

'It's a bloody long way, too.'

'*Ilhamdillah!*'

'Don't swear at me!'

Another time Lian said in frustration, 'People are the same everywhere. Why can't one be at home anywhere?'

'Of course people are the same. That has nothing to do with it. You go over there and you'll see that, but then it will be *too late*.' Phi-Van was cold, thin-voiced, shaking. Lian was furious and walked away.

Every day Dr Qabbani increased Lian's wealth.

It started with the nouns. Strange dry objects at first, specimens. They seemed to have no sensual or labial connection with their meanings. She accepted them as a code, learned the decrypting techniques, accepting their disconnection from all feeling. Arabic was cold and lifeless but deeply interesting to dissect. The verbs were vague: weak, seeming at first like cheap string tying bundles together. But then certain knots and clots made nouns. Everything came from strings, thickened into veins, was either entrails of nouns or tools for moving their dead bits about. Dr Qabbani handed them over as if they were the frozen moments of something infinitely beautiful, infinitely sad. Her manner more than the words themselves intrigued Lian.

The first word to ring a bell of its own meaning in her head was *asfar* or *safra*, masculine and feminine yellows. For a moment language was incarnated, then it became code again.

It was in second year that she saw the first stirrings of life in her oldest nouns. They had lain in her throat and dropped lifeless from her tongue countless times.

They fell now, briefly, and then fluttered off like awkward fledglings, powering directionless and out of control through the air. A bird, a sparrow, *usfour*, birds *asafiir*, seemed to float like yellow butterflies, birds of paradise or coral fish leaping from their glottal first consonant into flight. Dr Qabbani smiled. Lian was entranced. In Arabic there is no relationship between *bird* and *yellow* but Lian's first living words bled into each other and yellow coloured many and brought them to life on the wings of imaginary birds. *Safara*: to travel.

She polished each word at first, lovingly, and was rewarded with the slow patina and then deep glow. She moved to polishing phrases, struggling through the rhythms of lines of poetry, so beautiful, unpalatable and unattainable that she felt like crying. Dr Qabbani repeated them to her and God's language rolled glimmering and warm from her tongue and throat. Lian tried. The words huddled stickily together, halted at her lips and then fell from the cliff face stoically, again and again, like lemming army troops. Regimented, uniformed. Dr Qabbani's poetry wheeled on thermals in a blue sky, pulsing wings in the warm air, powerful, shining, richly coloured. Red as rubies, gold topaz, hot blue lapis lazuli.

In her dreams her voice also made the colours and she flew on the updraught of her own breath. She looked up *umm* in the dictionary. She knew the word well. Mother, one of the first words she had learned. Mother, source, origin, foundation, basis, original, essence.

Umma: Community.

Once she could converse she found that she had something to offer Dr Qabbani in return. Their classes had been crippled by the menagerie of limping words without meanings, stillborn phrases and a state of panicked deafness that set in as soon as something was too rich and fast to be grasped. She dreaded her honours year for she was the only student continuing and she could sense the pressure against her ears, on her lips and tongue long before the term started. But in honours she began to exchange meanings in Arabic and went home each day in a trance. They spoke about Australia.

'What is Easter celebrating?'

Lian was startled. How could one not know?

'The death and resurrection of Isa.'

They spoke about festivals. She knew even less about Islamic holidays than Dr Qabbani did about Australian ones.

Each day she collected, wrote about and discussed ordinary and bizarre Australian history and customs and Dr Qabbani found stranger equivalents for them in Sudanese culture and Arab history.

Easter and the Eid al-Adha

Steeples and minarets

Aussie battlers and tenacious peasants

White settlement and the Israelis

The Kelly Gang and bedouin raiders

'Look!' Lian said on graduation day. 'Australia looks Arab!'

'A bit Saudi, but Arab enough.'

*One day, as Abdallah of the Land reclined on the
sand in a gem-encrusted robe and Abdallah of
the Sea lay back in the shallows pulsing his broad
tail up and down, rolling a lemon between his
hands, the Merman turned to his friend and said,
'I would be honoured if you would visit my
home under the sea. I would like to show you the
submarine domains and how we live. You could
be my guest for a month or two.'*

She met a woman in the art gallery who had honey gold
skin and black eyes. She was named Rawya. Rawya was
from Yemen. 'I am the only Yemeniya in Australia,' she
said laughing. 'You must go and study Arabic in Yemen.
The Yemenis speak the dialect closest to the classical.
You cannot know Arabic until you have studied there.'

Rawya described for Lian a peaceful, green paradise:
Sanaa, the first city of the known world, the created,
invented, made. Torn of late by a smallish civil war,
just resolved. *La shiy laha*: nothing to it, nothing to
worry about.

mafeesh mushkila

Rawya hadn't been there since childhood.

Lian was filled with desire. She knew that she had to
go to the Middle East for the sake of her Arabic. In Yemen,
land of the dialect closest to the classical, Arabia Felix, no-
one spoke English and she would be forced to use her
Arabic. But really she chose Yemen because no-one had
heard of it and she was enchanted by Rawya's name.

Lian, Phi-Van and Nev had different kinds of rage.

Every time Lian got a little bit angry, Nev became exuberant and loving. 'Oh, it's you!' his face seemed to say, in happy surprise. Lian would try to seem angry for him as often as she could.

Phi-Van's brow looked as hard as skinless bone. It was ivory with rage. Nev's blood pulsed through thick veins, snaking down his temples. His rage was the more usual colour. His veins and colour rose and subsided, flooded and drained, tides sucked by the moon under Phi-Van's hairline. Lian simply retreated. She hid her self where not even she could find it. The three of them were pulsing, shining and retreating with rage a lot in the last few months before Lian left for Yemen.

Lian allowed herself to resent the tyranny of Phi-Van's terrible history.

Phi-Van never mentioned it. She didn't have to.

She told Dr Qabbani that she planned to go to Yemen.

'Yemen is very traditional, very backward,' her teacher said. 'The purest Arabic is spoken in the Sudan. You could stay with my family, and then your family would not worry about you.'

She protested that Dr Qabbani's family were so educated they would speak English with her.

'As you wish. At least in Yemen you will be safe.'

Dr Qabbani was the only person to say that to her.

'Oh my God, how sweet your Arabic!' The girl at the Yemen Airways counter in Cairo laughed. 'You speak like someone from the age of the Prophets!'

Lian hesitated momentarily as she broke the sentence up and put it back together again. Yes, that was really what the girl had said. She was disconcerted. She had been proud of the fluid beauty of her sentence, at the liquid, warm sound of 'Is it possible to take these bags with me in the plane?'. Her moon letters and sun letters had all been immaculate.

The girl smiled at her, asking where she had studied Arabic, why she was going to Yemen, and checked forty kilos in as baggage.

'Oh, but in Egypt we speak the purest Arabic, the closest to the literary, the classical. You should stay and study here!' Then, saving Lian from her confusion and tongue-tied shuffling for an apology for passing up Egypt: 'God bless your journey!'

She thought, a few weeks later, how polite that girl had been. Her Arabic was horrible, even to her own ears.

Abdallah of the Land made a polite apology, astounded that the Merman did not know that a Landsman would drown under the sea. The Merman laughed and said, 'Oh, don't worry about that!' and he dived under the water and disappeared. Abdallah of the Land waited uncertainly, stood up and dusted the sand off his embroidered cloak. Was he supposed to follow as a foolish gesture of trust and commitment to his friend? What was the correct thing to do? Just as he began to touch the water with his toe, the Merman popped up again carrying a large pink shell shaped like a twist of a woman's hair.

'Take off all your clothes,' he commanded, handing the shell to his friend. Abdallah of the Land felt foolish but he did as his friend requested. He stood naked in front of the Merman, holding the shell in both his hands.

'In the shell is the fat of the Dandan fish,' said the Merman. 'Coat yourself from head to toe in it and you will be as one of us under the sea!'

Abdallah of the Land poked the contents of the shell. It was filled with a soft, smooth substance, yellow and clear as oil, perfumed with a scent he couldn't recognise. He began to cloak himself with it, surprised by the pleasant tingling sensation against his skin. The Merman watched him until he finished, smiled and said, 'Follow me!' and dived under the rising swell.

'Phi-Van's a softie, really.' Nev's voice had a slightly pleading note and Lian flicked her hair out of her eyes, annoyed. They were standing out in the wild oats on a late summer night, watching moonrise over the black bay. Lian was home for the holidays and Phi-Van was locked in her room after a tense first evening. They had sat together at dinner. Nev looked old to Lian and he and Phi-Van seemed strangely eccentric, as if they were the last two people left on earth and had only each other. The greeting at the ferry started it all. Phi-Van had looked her up and down, running her eye up the long tanned legs and the muscled shoulders. She frowned.

'Lian, a girl your age should have a space between her inner thighs. You must lose weight. When I was your age, I was a size 8.'

Lian had looked her mother up and down, the mirror insult. But words died on her lips. Unstated, the story hung in the air between them. *Where were you, Phi-Van, at nineteen? Eating a handful of rice a day, then losing everything to sit, hugging the knobs of bony knees under torn pink cotton, huddled on the garboard strake of an open boat.*

The light in the kitchen was too dim, she noticed. It had always been the same, but it seemed to have lost lustre. It cast dingy shadows into uncleaned corners and she realised suddenly that Phi-Van had stopped house-keeping. The kitchen was Nev through and through.

Everything she said all evening Phi-Van met with silence or with icy monosyllables.

'If you say so,' Lian finally said to Nev, meaning to

say nothing. Nev said nothing in return and the moon rose, picking out the fierce glitter of the still sea.

'If rocks are soft,' she murmured, and he heard. He turned to her, his big shoulders hunching. He raised his hands up into the shape of a small melon in front of her face.

'She's a *baby*, Lian. With a skull of eggshells.'

Lian watched the moon through his hands, filling the gentle cups of his paws to the brim. She had looked closely at her mother that evening. Nev, as always, had had his hands on Phi-Van — on her shoulders, on her waist, touching her cheek; and, as always, Phi-Van was stiff under the caresses, ungiving. But distance and time showed up something that Lian had not noticed before. Nev's hands seemed to make Phi-Van, to confirm her in place, to define her and even hold her in existence. She could see the hands reassuring, rebuilding her mother with every touch, as though without this, that stiff form would melt away and be gone altogether. It was the last thing Lian wanted to see or know. Phi-Van's face was smooth and impassive but now Lian saw clearly that it was frozen into the faintest flinch, pulling one eye awry and the mouth stiff with fear or sadness. Lian had wanted to slap it. She pictured her own tiny head in Nev's luminous palm and decided then, in the glittering grass and the rising night wind, never again to return home. She could not bear this again.

SWIMMING IN SANAA

She yanked on the old, yellow wetsuit and spat into her goggles. She greased her forehead and cheekbones with vaseline to make the badly fitting mask seal and then pressed it against her face. It made a sighing and then snorting sound as it suckered on. She fiddled with the weight belt, tightened the buoyancy jacket, checked the air release and hauled loud mouthfuls of air through the thin pipes from the tank. Click. Rush. Click. The sounds of an operating theatre, of the invalid and incapacitated. She stumbled across the deck, bent slightly to carry the weight of the tank and belt, awkward inside her braced and stiffened form, and heating up rapidly with each movement. With her back to the ocean she slowly wrenched her fins onto her feet and tightened the straps behind her ankles. Her fingers fumbled, the blood supply constricted by the wetsuit, the enforced slowness of her movements making her limbs lethargic. She stuck the tattered 'diver below' flag into the fishing rod holder. Then she rolled backwards and smashed into the water, curled like a beetle and striking exoskeleton first.

The ocean closed over her head and, except for the lone burble of her muffled breathing, silence was instant. She sank slowly into the blue, making insect clicks in her skull as she pressed minute bubbles of air into her ears. Her body shrank slightly in the suit, melded with it rather than pushing against it, and she changed, as she had many times before, into a warm and weightless creature. She stopped three metres from the bottom, hovering motionless, held alive and flying in the beautiful land beneath the world. The blue enveloped her and the birds of the water darted in and out of their trees and crevices. The light rippled along her pale gold body as she moved and she felt an inner sealion ease radiating past her fluorescent and metallic form. She swam along the side of the reef to the drop-off, descending. Her green hair floated back and forth with each stroke of the fins, tossed by the alien silver globules that tore distorted from her mouthpiece, then rotated, formed shimmering spheres and rushed towards the distant, upside-down skin of blue-silver far above. Her own acoustic signature rang its dreamlike tinkles along her form, a chant in eerie whispers which resonated through her body to her inner ear.

She powered steadily around the cliff face of the reef, fins moving in unison. Her forehead dove first and the ripple seemed to pass in a wave along her clumsy jointed body, but really her fins, alternately pressing the water upward then feeling its resistance downward, propelled her almost elegantly through the luminous sea.

The fish thinned and the striated whiskers of the crays were gone before she reached their holes and crevices. She turned upward and swam over the cliff rim into the deep pools, clefts and eddies on the land side of the small rocky island. Tiny fish darted in and out of havens in the corals, weeds, rocks, old shells, stones and gem-encrusted bones. The big fish were nowhere to be seen.

She felt a change in the water and at the same moment something large, green and shadowy rushed towards her from behind her head. She felt it. By the time she had spun to face the deep, it was twirling away from her, large and indistinct, dimming rapidly. Her heart beat wildly and she could hear herself drawing heavily at her air. It couldn't be a shark; they didn't move that way. It had swum away as if following the path of a gymnast's ribbon. A sealion. Sealion. She stared out into the blue with desire stiffening her ribs, waiting. It didn't return. She glided slowly up a wide ravine, lined on both sides with intensifying colour, glittering more and more brightly as she rose nearer to the surface. The blues and greens of the deeper palisades yellowed, and from the blackest blues emanated purple, then dimmed reds. The transition was so slow that yellow was upon her

before she was aware, herself part of the slow magic of
rising to the light. Her own flesh lightened to a shadow
of warmth. She came up level with a cleft in the high
cliffs of the reef, the entrance to the deep pool. She
caught her breath and then eased it through the
mouthpiece with the care of a wild animal. The pool was
full of sealions, swimming, floating, playing around a
central group who were dancing a sealions' corroboree. A
sealion party. She held very still in the water about ten
metres away from them. Young sealions and female
sealions made helix paths towards her and then flipped
back on their trails and sped away. Their sleek bodies
glimmered in the dancing waterlights. She adjusted her
buoyancy furtively until she hung in the water, suspend-
ed a metre above the rock, rising gently as she breathed
in and sinking again as she breathed out. The sealions
danced above her, unperturbed. Some lay in stiff arcs in
the water, belly up, fins pushed through the skin of the
surface and held rigid in the breeze above. Their large
eyes were black holes rimmed with waterlight. Others
performed slow sideways arcs, raising single flippers in a
slicing motion through the silver surface, one side then
the other, making distended infinity signs. Some young
seals had their feet out of the water, looking oddly as if
they were standing on their hands. They craned their
heads around to watch the others and twisted their
flaptoes, which hung in the wind like leathery leaves of
some just-sprung seedling. Little sealions wove in and
out amongst the statues of their relatives and shot

94

through the skin whole, only to land with graceless irruptions, bombing into the thick of the serene dancers. One, and then all, started shooting out of the water backwards, seen indistinctly through the silver borderline, their forms glittery and fragmented, sailing through the air far above and crashing back home like ragdolls.

A male cruised past in the deep behind her, his great ruff glittering pale gold in the filtered light. She stayed still in the water, her heart leaping. She was caught at the threshold of silliness and grace, her meccano limbs forgotten, her metallic beetle back gone, waiting for the moment when they would reach out and beckon her, calling her into the heart of light.

Her breathing became laboured of its own accord. At the moment when she glanced at her gauges, she ran out of air and had to make an emergency ascent on her last lungful.

She never saw them again, although she went there several times to look. She saw them often in her dreams. She became a sealion, sometimes, and they welcomed her home, the long-lost wanderer. Other times she hovered, awkward, and they looked through her. Other times she swam insistently up to them and they scattered in panic and the sea filled with blood.

Enter another culture and you will fall apart, assailed by something, unsupported, having to know alone who you are without the recognition of those around you. We are all read in the flicker of the eye; we are turned like pages in the palms of passers-by and well-fingered, even dog-eared by our family and circle. Enter another culture and you become a simple, flat and lonely cipher: the outsider, the incomprehensible. Wear the clothes, walk the walk, make yourself smaller or larger, mimic the syllables and you will discover your loneliness. Hold yourself tight, button your Levis with steady fingers, make an image of intact otherness out of yourself, it makes no difference: unread, unopened, you cease to mean anything beyond your skin and fabric covers.

Phi-Van had frozen, to prevent further assault and loss.

Lian, however, found that a person with delayed feelings is a very fragile thing. She was taken by surprise. Firstly, new feelings were upon her with uncommon rapidity; and, secondly, none of her versions of herself were relevant. She, who had preplanned and prepared for everything, went around with pricked ears, waiting to hear from others who she might begin to be and shocked at how raw what was left of her felt.

Who is she?
al-Siniya
al-Ustraliya
Muslima
Masihiya
Marreh Yemeni
Sitt al-Qisas

Everyone knew her and dismissed her in these chunky labels. The shopkeepers and fruit-sellers, street children and dogs were used to her strange stride and peculiar, preconsidered classical Arabic. She had become almost unremarkable, a quotidian outsider.

The Australian. The Chinese. A Muslim. A Christian. The wife of a Yemeni. The Lady of Stories.

Mashallah Mashallah. This she heard, too. The words, with their intensity and indirectness, made her chest swell with a stormy happiness. She understood these words that didn't stay inside rules of meaning.

Whatever God wills, meaning, *I am beautiful.*

In Sanaa, you sought the company of women. But Sanaa had a reflective meniscus that was more than the wall the black *sharashif* and *balto* put up. Women deflected all attempts to know them, ensconced in private worlds that needed no penetration. They needed no outside observer to recognise themselves, for they were home. Lian found herself looking on, for months, then looking inward. The women around her were hidden behind silver refractions but Phi-Van swam between her palms in a tiny aquarium. The more she looked at Sanaa and hoped hopelessly for acceptance, the more she thought of her mother.

One by one her senses deserted her. It was as if the

world around her, colourful, complex and mysterious, was leaching away everything she had.

Phi-Van sunk her white fingers into Lian's arms, pinning her. She lifted the child up onto a chair, picked up each ankle and folded Lian's legs, methodically tucking all the bits away into a small bundle. Her face was smooth but Lian could tell she was mad. Phi-Van was sometimes very calm when she was angry. Calm and far away. Phi-Van crossed the small arms around the bony knees, attaching hands to shoulders. Then she tucked the dress in neat hospital corners around Lian's bottom, took Lian's head between her hands and carefully centred it.

Thus packaged, Lian knew she was not to move. After an hour she whimpered slightly but stopped when Phi-Van turned slowly towards her, standing still for seconds with her hands full of noodle glue. Under the strange gaze of her mother, she froze.

When Nev unpacked her eight hours later, he had to massage her body back into movable parts. He said nothing, either to her or Phi-Van. He kneaded her back, neck and buttocks with his huge, gentle hands, singing softly in a motherly voice: whale tunes just for her ears. For a long time after that Lian went with Nev if she had to stay home from school or if he went away on weekends. Phi-Van said nothing. It was as if she didn't remember.

She let herself in, watched by dogs, an old man, three passing young women and two tiny boys who had halted momentarily a game with a plastic bottle threaded lengthways as a wheel on the end of a long wire. The old man knew of her. The *ajnabiya*, they're all crazy. The young women asked each other:

Is she engaged to a Yemeni yet?

She spoke a long time with Hassan the Attar.

But she was with the Russian. The Russian always speaks a long time to the Attar.

She will marry an educated man.

Very educated.

The boys watched to see if she would give something to the dogs. Foreigners were funny about dogs. She didn't. Once she was gone and her steps had faded into the interior, they played and shouted again, wheeling the clacking contraption in enticing arcs. The old man lowered his head and walked down the lane. The young women headed for the market chattering in sotto voce gaiety, their fluted black cloths fluttering as they walked.

Lian watched them from the carved blue-green door inset into the third-floor shutter. Very few people accepted her as more than a familiar exotic: the archetypal oddity, a party livener. She slowly unwound the *hijab* and opened her embroidered black *balto*. These days she floated easily through the streets. She could feel

the gentle exploratory nudges of goodwill reaching out
and buoying her up, assisting her with warm currents of
simple one-word recognitions.

Lian met Abha at Sanaa University. Abha was twenty-
nine, studying for her masters in community medicine.
When they met, Abha was covered except for her eyes.
She placed a soft gloved hand on Lian's arm one day and
asked her where she was from. Even at the time, Lian's
heart beat faster. From the unseen face she heard the
sweet syllables of interest and friendliness directed at
her alone.

Abha lifted the veil covering her eyes, and Lian was
in the warm glow of beauty and subtle need. Abha
wanted to know her.

Abha's *balto* was well cut, stylish, unadorned and
of a very fine light material. She moved with grace,
maqrama floating slightly behind her, its crossed
triangles overlapping like the feathers on a bird's back.
A piece of the *litham*, much like a black bridal veil, could
be pulled forward, covering even her eyes. Lian felt like
an oafish, oversized and poorly dressed redneck,
striding next to Abha. Something in the grace and
fluidity of Abha's movements made Lian buy a more
stylish *balto* for herself and try for a more feminine
image. There was not much she could do about her feet,
for no Yemeniya had size nines.

Abha invited her to a *tafrita*, a women's party.

She dressed for the *tafrita* with care. Long blue silk dress, a present from Phi-Van, black high-heeled shoes, perfume. She hid herself in her *balto* and *hijab* and waited for the car to pick her up. Abha's brother Ibrahim didn't speak to her or look at her. He drove the car, ferrying and apparently ignoring his sister's friends.

Lian was met inside the door of a modern house by a gaunt young woman with huge black eyes, who grasped her hand and murmured conventional welcomes in Abha's low voice. Lian tried not to be shaken, but she was embarrassed and caught in the curiosity of discovery. Abha was an emaciated version of her brother, and, where he gave off lassitude, she was strung with tension. Abha was very beautiful but, she said, old in the company of the girls at the party and excluded from the circle of married women and mothers. Her mane of black hair was piled up and then fell in curlicues around her shoulders, leaving her forehead bare. She was dressed in a tailored off-the-shoulder dress of majenta silk which showed her collarbone strung like a drawn bow under the skin. Lian was startled until they entered the vestibule leading to the *mafraj*. Girls and women were ranged in front of the mirror, teasing hair and tweaking garish and brilliant dresses sequinned and beaded in excessive patterns, taffetas, silks, bright chiffons floating over satin. Shimmer, glitter and glory in every colour filled the hall and the *mafraj* and Lian suddenly realised that her best was very plain, as was

Abha's. Lian's sheer cut, loose silk was very out of fashion here.

More and more women and girls poured noisily into the room, laughing, the young girls sliding glances sideways to see whose mother or sisters were looking. Lian was entranced. Yemeni women seemed to her beautiful, happy and confident, and she wished she was one of them. Sisters entered, often dressed in the same fabric, sometimes five together with the youngest under ten and looking like a flowergirl. Sisters, cousins and friends fell noisily upon each other, exclaiming in high fluid voices on subjects Lian could rarely catch.

Someone approached her and stopped beside her, and Lian turned from the door. Abha was next to her, leaning down and holding out a tiny glass of hot red tea. The majenta shone against the warm, rounded skin of the extended arm and Lian jumped. This was not Abha at all. Smiling into her face was a full, round and happy version of Ibrahim and Abha's faces, the mouth generous and the striking eyes gentle. She looked much younger than either of them.

'I am Ammat al-Rahman, Abha's sister.'

Ammat al-Rahman moved on, serving the tea to the glittering host and soon disappeared in the throng. Lian caught at glances and phrases eddying about her, trying through the fog of rising tension to decode both.

Part of the point of the *tafrita* was to see and to be seen. Everyone was performer and viewer in a spectator sport, chatting to friends and checking out everyone who came in. Soon the room was full and women settled in clusters, chewing qat and smoking the *mada'a*, smoke filling air which was heady with incense and countless perfumes. Near Lian, a middle-aged woman with a broad laughing face, pink lipstick and a hot pink, overtight dress with gathered skirt clapped her hands and shouted. The three girls in green next to Lian, who had been eyeing her with friendly shyness, leaned to her and whispered suddenly in unison, *'al-Duktura Bahija!'*

Doctor Bahija called loudly for music, and the room hushed to whispers as Abha appeared, *Ud* in hand, and began to tune it.

'She is of the Malikis,' the green girls whispered excitedly and Lian for some reason heard them clearly. The threads of the music, both melancholy and detached at the same time, calmed Lian and drew her into the room with the others. Abha was bowed over the instrument, her face unreadable and her body quivering with the chords she plucked. The *Ud* was a golden fruit in her lap, touched as if a baby one second and then torn by her flying fingers as if being eviscerated in refined and steely steps. *Ud* was sand, mountains, sea and sky, with the pain of human life threaded through unalloyed and unregarded. The stuffy room vanished, the puffs of smoke from the *madaa* becoming as distant as the wind devils that twirled dust across the Sanaa plateau, dancing between the mountains. Abha shook and spun their known world for them and they sighed with the sadness and the joy of being shown it.

And Lian, seeing this, feeling it, was all the more the outsider.

The playing ended abruptly. Abha stood and left the room with a sudden smile, returning to her role as host. A small tape player was switched on and blared tinny travesties of *Ud* and voice into the room. Young girls danced in tandem and everyone began shouting and laughing again.

An imprecise sadness settled like ash on Lian but her strain and embarrassment didn't return. She was driven home a couple of hours later by Ammat al-Rahman.

Lian moved out of the student house with Helena, who was working now for a German archaeologist, searching for another elusive Yemeniya, the Queen of Sheba. Her second house was just around the corner and down an alley from the Taj Talha hotel, in what at first seemed a labyrinthine part of the old walled city. She and Helena kept the huge house alone for a month. Ana had vanished into Yemeni society, staying in a succession of Yemeni houses and visiting now and then. Lian envied and admired Ana's ability with people but could not duplicate it. Ana, armed with a little Arabic, *hijab* and *balto*, had flung herself into Yemeni life with an unquestioning love for people and experiences. Ana used every single word or gesture at her disposal and was invited all over the country to weddings, *tafritas* and qat chews.

Ana was simply beloved by all, Yemeni and foreigner alike.

Then Kobe wanted to move in with them. Kobe was tall, elegant, pale blonde. She dressed as a Yemeniya would, but always with enough blonde showing at the fringe to be dramatically noticeable. She had a thin crust of impeccable manners. Her Arabic was very good. She had slipped into Yemen with ease, accepting with regal grace all assistance offered to a presumed feminine helplessness. Within a week she had a job as a tour guide, was intimate friends with the American ambassador's daughter, had obtained the unobtainable private lessons at the Language School and was living with a Yemeni family. This last, everyone's dream, was what she was dissatisfied with.

Helena and Lian were enchanted by her calm voice, soothing manners, and pressured by her need. Kobe spoke Arabic, English, Swedish and German, and promised contacts with Yemeni women and their elusive households. So the house by the Taj became known for the tall blonde woman, the sweet German, and the strange Chinese. Helena, Lian and Kobe lived in their crooked house, their salon, like picnickers at the seaside.

The house was six storeys tall and looked out over a *miqshama*, or public garden, and a *hammam*. From the *mafraj*, the *miqshama* looked like Rapunzel's garden.

It was laid out in plots of well-tended radishes and spring onions, surrounded by peppercorn trees and then the high façades of decorated houses. The water from the public bath flowed in channels around the garden, as it had for centuries. Straight down below, white lilies grew in a prow shape leading away from the house wall where there had once been a composting toilet with a drop of five floors.

The façade of Lian's house had a comical air. The house was too twisted and off-perpendicular to look serious about itself. It steadied itself on both neighbouring houses. Its sills and elaborate friezes had been recently renovated and stood out stark white against the soft faun of the mudbrick. It looked as though dressed for a corroboree. The upper storeys almost made a face, the eyes wide with startled clown-drops in white diamonds above them, white lashes. It was staring at something it could not believe.

Inside, apart from a pink and mauve Western bathroom with a Western toilet, it was exotic, austere and peaceful. Lian's room was larger and more oblong than her last and had more windows. It was strangely quiet, with white walls lit as before with the slowly tracking patterned lights from the windows.

Her rooftop was level with the parapets of the Taj Talha hotel. From this eyrie, Sanaa stretched out in front of her, lovely and ancient. The tips of peppercorns and eucalypts reached up between the houses, the striated and patterned minarets reaching even further into the blue. The houses made layers and layers of arabesques filled with faint glittering glass — iced façades and a patterned, regular tapestry to the foot of the dry mountains. From this height it looked exquisite and, except for the satellite dishes, timeless. She thought for a moment that all rubbish was invisible but the white shape she had mistaken for the moon rotated and became square. A plastic bag, high on a thermal, hovered with the kites over the city.

Abdallah's scalp crawled with terror as he dived into the sea.

He waited for the terrible tightness of the chest, the claustrophobic clutch of the cruel and rapacious ocean. Eyes clenched, he waited, drifting downwards. Then he felt a gentle touch on his hand and opened his eyes. He could see as clearly as ever. The blue-green light was ribbed over his friend's face. Abdallah the Merman was peering up at him, swimming with languid grace beneath him. His own limbs felt light and free and silken, cushioned by the soft ebb and flow of the currents. His chest was moving up and down, a current of water jetting from his nostrils with each breath, but he felt no pain or fear. He looked at his aquamarine body shimmering and ribbed too with bands of light. He stared at his friend's laughing face with wonder.

'We are your people and we say no!' Helena said laughing, flourishing an arm in a grandiose Arab woman's gesture. They were all gathered in the *mafraj* of the Taj house.

Ana looked wanly amused. Then she laughed but it was as if she was laughing at something private.

Lian looked at her closely.

'If he had no other wife, would you have said yes?'

Ana smiled wryly through sudden tears.

They had all been treating it as a joke. Ana's friend Ahmad had asked her to become his second wife. It wasn't a cultural ambush: they had known each other for years. It wasn't a terrible misunderstanding on her part, although it seemed to have been on his. Lacking the confidence to ask his university friend to marry him, he had bowed to family pressure and married his cousin instead, a year ago.

Now for some reason his passion had topped over his reserve, and he had asked.

'Tell him that where you come from the man must be a virgin!'

'Tell him we, your people, say no!'

'Bloody cheek! What does he take you for?'

Lian had met Ahmad. A tiny boy-man with dark eyes, high eyebrows, a soft but resonant voice and exquisite, ageless manners. He had something of the old bedouin stereotype: face like a hunting bird, eyes of a gazelle, night black hair, a wiry form and the reassuring gentleness of an innate hospitality and respect for others. Ahmad looked her in the eye for the length of his handshake. He did not hesitate in extending his hand to a woman. He was twenty-five but already carried the responsibilities of his tribe. He was some sort of sedentary chief. He was educated in Germany but had forgotten his German as rapidly as he had learned it.

Ana had always called him her Yemeni brother. He had called himself her Yemeni brother. However, when he wrote to Germany to tell her of his plans to marry his first wife he had been hoping for her objection not her congratulations.

Helena suddenly stopped laughing. She saw Lian's thoughtful face and realised that Ana was sobbing.

'You were tempted!' she said, her blue eyes widening. For all Helena's love of Yemen, love for a Yemeni had never occurred to her as possible.

'Just have an affair with him!'

Ana started like a sensitive horse reined in and whipped in the same moment.

Helena recoiled. She said apologetically, self-effacingly, 'Marrying a married man is *not* the same as having an affair with a married man.'

They were all silent. It was frightening that Ana had none of the intangible barriers between herself and a Yemeni friend. But she had misunderstood his message at a crucial moment, too.

She said that she had been in love with him since she was sixteen.

The four women sat around the table helpless. Ana

cried softly and Lian put her arms around the small shoulders awkwardly, as she imagined a mother would comfort a child. Yemen seemed to Lian suddenly much more serious, more scarring than she had thought it to be, and, at the same time, she noticed that *she had always known this*, and that she had hoped it would, even if against her will, scratch her until she bled.

Ana said that her parents were coming to take her home. Lian felt a strange sense of bereavement. Having Ana somewhere silly and happy and immersed in Yemen had strengthened her. And, without Ana, who around her was succeeding?

*At first the land under the sea was a wilderness.
They passed through forests of weed filled with
fish, bright yellow, purple, blue, orange, green,
and silver schools he would have dreamed of
netting. They might just as easily have been birds
or butterflies. The fronds and tendrils of the plants
were so light that they waved to and fro at the
slightest movement in the water. Abdallah of the
Land looked about him. He looked up and realised
that the shimmering surface was remote above
him. They were deeper under the sea than the
length of two minarets. The sun was like a green
flower, or a coin seen in a stream. Suddenly they
reached the end of the wilds and he saw that they
were at the edge of a great ocean valley. Gardens
and terraces of corals stretched as far as he could*

see to either side. At the bottom a city lay spread out, glittering with green and blue lights. Other lights were moving near them, travelling along the road, and suddenly a host of the sea people were upon them. Abdallah the Merman greeted them in the name of God and they returned his greeting. They flowed around the two friends and went on their way. They were all very similar, with glowing faces of striking beauty and long tails instead of legs. They were naked, he noticed, even the women.

'Do you all go about naked?' he asked, his astonishment evident in his voice.

'God made us so,' the Merman said quietly, not wishing to distress his friend. 'Besides, look down: you too are naked here, my friend!'

Abdallah looked down at his body, floating behind him. He had forgotten that he too was naked and he blushed greenly under the sea. But his friend was moving on and he soon forgot about his body again.

'Shall we enter that lovely city?' he asked, pointing.

'Under the sea, you must not point,' the Merman said mildly. 'Those desiring alliances with Lacktails used the finger pointed towards the surface as a sign. Wave instead, so!' He flourished his long fingered hand. 'And yes, that small village is my home and we will enter it eventually. But

*first I wish to show you some of the wonders of
our world.'*

*I am a Lacktail here, thought Abdallah of the
Land to himself. Not a Havelegs. He felt humbled,
momentarily, but knew that he would never want
to exchange his smooth legs for a slimy tail.*

Abha's brother Ibrahim took Lian and Helena to a
wedding dance at the Wadi Dahr. This time he chatted,
catching their eyes in the rear-vision mirror, giving them
quick glimpses of his own black eyes and arched
eyebrows. He told them a little about himself, asked
them about themselves and managed to make a much
better impression than on the night of the *tafrita*. Lian
decided that he wasn't so much unfriendly as pre-
occupied. Ibrahim was a tribesman, a *qabili*, who was
waiting in Sanaa for his visa to do his PhD in America.
He already had a scholarship but without a visa he could
not take it up and in a few months it would expire. He
wanted to speak English but they wanted to speak
Arabic, so he obliged. He smiled at them once, in the
mirror, and Lian was startled. He looked very young,
with such white teeth and shining eyes. She asked him
how old he was. He said, 'Much too old,' and she was
unsure, suddenly, if he was saying something else. She
was confused too by a sad note in his voice and
something wooden about him and wondered whether
her Arabic was really good enough to pick up sad notes
and woodiness. She lapsed into silence, listening with

half an ear to Ibrahim and Helena chatting, and staring out the window at the bleak, thorny hillsides.

The dance ledge was a huge jutting rock, several hundred square metres across, leaning out over a wide valley filled with qat plantations and almost camouflaged villages. The dancers were raising dust from the centre of a crowd but were obscured by the layers of people, children, cars and picnickers. The scene recalled a country race meeting: festive, gregarious. The lined-up dusty and battered Ladas or lightly dinged Monicas and Laylas looked not so different from a collection of old Falcons, Kingswoods and landholders' 4WDS.

Lian's spirits lifted. The air was charged with the celebration and light-heartedness that goes with serious events that can be made lovely only for a day. Once out of the car, she could hear the music and the clapping, and a sighing pulse that seemed to come up from the rock itself — the beat of many feet in the dust. She tightened her *hijab* about her neck and pulled her *balto* around her, overwhelmed by the crowd, wanting to be invisible so she could enjoy the heady excitement. She could feel Ibrahim's eyes on her, just the first in line of many eyes, if she turned to look. She wished she had worn a *litham*. She wished he would leave them to wander alone at their own pace and, suddenly, he did.

'Go to the edge and watch!' he shouted in English, smiling once again. He made off into the crowd and Lian and Helena turned to the cliff-top wedding dancers.

The dance was both hypnotically choreographed and impromptu. Anyone could join in, if male, and young men continually leapt into the ring to dance as apprentices or to show their skill. The circle of men danced a halting somehow clumsy and somehow graceful measure, their steps shaking the dust into small clouds about their ankles. Each raised one arm in the air, clutching the horn, wood or silver hilts of their *jambiyas*. The blades made strange airy movements, slicing in slow arcs like wings or the fins of fish, catching the sunlight in sudden flashes, triangular gleams. Their hands and blades moved every which way, random but ordered, glittering like a descant above the more determined bobbing heads with their soiled grey, spotted red, pure white *mshaddas*. The men danced around the bridegroom and the children squealed in the dust. The rock jutted out over the valley. Kites wheeled.

Suddenly Ibrahim was there in the dance; and there, in the company of men, Lian saw him as he might have been, might be, even. His raised arm was a flashing curve of brown muscle and sinew, the sleeve of the *kamis* slipping down a little to reveal a fine curved line to wrist and hilt. His hand movements were captivating: they were almost still and the blade moved in a slow arc, but they had a line of grace and power. She realised that, while his wrists were very fine, his hands were large. His body shook with his stamping, his chest broad but supple through the shoulders, his hips lean and narrow, with the empty *jambiya* scabbard shaking on the ornate belt with each step. She had thought him smaller than herself, but there, dancing in the company of men, she saw that he was tall: tall and lean and beautiful, with the grace of a bird, with the fine limbs of the gazelle and the broad chest.

Lian's heart soared with the dance but seemed to flutter and smash high up against a glass barrier between herself and the sky. She was both very happy and very miserable and could not work out why. She tried to pretend later that she had only been the one.

She glanced at Ibrahim's face as he danced on the far edge of the cliff top. He looked fierce and distant and happy, as if he really was soaring. Something hurt in her chest and she looked away. She did not look at him again.

Lian wrote to Phi-Van after the dance, describing the flashing blades and the slow, sure movements. She knew that Phi-Van would see blood on the blades and aggression rather than concentration in the faces she painted. She knew but wrote it anyway.

This is my natural home, my spiritual home, she wrote, ardently, but knowing that it would hurt.

Your mother misses you, Nev wrote in one of his curt and stilted cards. Lian was suddenly very angry. Nev did not call Phi-Van a *mother*. Phi-Van herself winced at the word.

Fi-Mum Fi-Mum Fi Fo Fi Fum: that was her name before Lian could say Phi-Van.

Phi-Van was filled with terror with the birth of her daughter. This made her terrifying: the bright, hard, clinging, resentful, neglectful mother.

Phi-Van had stood beleaguered when Lian was a toddler. Lian stalked her with Nev's help, both of them laughing and shrieking like fruit bats from behind flimsy table legs. Phi-Van retreated into the bone room in her head and added the child's sunhat to the strange collection at the bottom of her wardrobe.

It was a relief when it came. It was always a relief. The explosion of physical violence was cleaner, simpler, than the build-up of prohibitions, petty cruelties and humiliations. The image of Phi-Van erect, elegant, wielding whatever weapons were within reach, and Lian, cowed, her greater bulk bent before her mother's onslaught, stuck in Lian's mind as the moment of truth between them, reasserted again and again after many lies, stripping away the accretion of layers of bravado or acrimony. After all but the last beating, all would be cleansed and easy between them, almost affectionate.

But that last time was different. At first, as blood rushed in her mouth with the shock and sweet rush of relief that the storm had finally broken, she felt herself as oafish, pathetic, deserving of these blows that she knew she had goaded, dared, invited from her mother. 'Slut, filth,' Phi-Van whispered, pulling her upright by her hair, and Lian let herself be pulled, helped, even, for Phi-Van was perhaps not strong enough to have lifted her had she gone completely limp. *Ugliness, barren, pride, dishonesty, worm.* These were her names. She did not need to listen. She was used to a satisfying quiescence, a humble, gleeful self-disgust but this time something else rose up as she stared between her knees, dreamy and quiet, the hulk of her body being battered somewhere far above. Suddenly she was angry. Why was she so cowardly that she took this pose, that she didn't straighten her huge body and at least take this standing up? What was she protecting in this private cocoon, guarding her head with her arms? Take it, calm, straight, immobile, or else ... with one blow from these great arms bash her mother's skull in. She didn't move out of the steps of their usual dance but her anger grew. *I am seventeen, not twelve!* She seethed and writhed inwardly as, bow-backed, she ducked and cowered. How great her own strength was! How pitiful to protect herself! How pathetic not to *use it*! How deformed her hunched submission.

Phi-Van was gasping, her strength leaving her as the welts rose on Lian's arms and shoulders. That one first blow to her face was suffused with purple. The scuba hoses fell from Phi-Van's hands. Lian knew that the arms would fall and her mother would stare at her without apology but in utter calm, soon, soon. But this

117

last time nothing settled, nothing unfurled or softly crept forth from Lian. Her anger rose and she cut herself loose from their shared pattern. When she finally rose, she was made taut and smooth by anger and in the end she raised a face to Phi-Van so terrible in its rage that Phi-Van ran from the room.

They passed a crowd dancing in wide circles
around flat rocks spread with shells and fish
of all sizes, colours and shapes. The sea people
were in pairs and trailed garlands of blue and
green seaweeds. Children sat at the fringes of the
group marshalling hundreds of small schools of
glow fish that darted this way and that,
illuminating the crowd.

'Is that a wedding?' Abdallah of the Land
asked.

'No! That is the first birthday feast!' Sure
enough in the centre of the biggest rock was
a clam with a baby asleep in it.

They swam on past villages and towns, the
Merman explaining all the while the wonders
that appeared on every side. Abdallah of the
Land became used to the people who swam by
and stared at him. He started to notice that some
of the women were bolder than others, and that
their glances searched for and held his gaze.
He felt both pleasure and discomfort at this and
was painfully aware of being naked before them.

'Do any of us ever marry any of you?' he
asked the Merman.
'Oh yes, on occasion. But it usually ends
badly!'
'How do you celebrate weddings?'
'With us, weddings are a private matter,
decided between the couple who wish to
live together.'
Abdallah of the Land was astounded but he
said nothing, for he didn't want to upset his friend.

It was early summer in Sanaa. Lian walked through the
cinnamon-reeking market on a bright morning, cool
blue sky aloof from the heat-sodden city. The stench
of donkey manure and the stench of crushed cardamom
and pepper mingled headily in the unstable cinnamon
air. She passed the old public fountain once built as
a Good Work, now dry and chained. The crowds
thickened and men passed her on both sides, preserv-
ing the magical centimetre of space for her to pass,
jostling and shoving at the perimeter of her cocoon
of air.

Just then, a hand shot up between her legs, fingers
clambering through the material, scrabbling as if
independent from an arm, leaping in fingerly bounds to
snatch at her. She flailed, scraping the world off her
body, spinning enraged onto a doe-faced young man
who was poised to flee. She screamed, *'Ya AIB! ya AIB!*
Shame on you!'

She was shaking, her body hot with revulsion. A riot broke out around the young man, *mshaddas* from everywhere converging around him, drowning him in cries of outrage. Dull thuds came from the vortex of swirling human anger. She looked on for a moment and then turned and strode away, weak and drained.

She told Helena and Kobe, and they each let off steam at Yemeni men. She had a shower. Alone in the *mafraj*, the breezes and eddies quietened to scented stillness, she was again suddenly shaking. She wondered if she would be able to see Yemen the same way again. She sat with her legs tightly crossed. It was a little thing, an ordinary, mean, little thing.

But in Yemen, she knew, it was a very big thing. She was angry again, a crossed legs angry. No Yemeniya would have to put up with that. But maybe, here in the city, they would. And when they chose to drop the cloth from their faces and laugh out loud at centuries of privacy and safety and silence? What then?

A wave washed over her and a fearful voice whispered: men are the opposite, the other, the outsider, the enemy at the door. Lian shored herself up, gaining strength, retreating and closing until she could be the impervious jelly rubber of an anemone. The phrase was repeated, with the firmness of a definition, a rule to live by. It had a familiar, even soothing timbre, spoken in a quiet resigned voice. Phi-Van's voice.

It was cast in Phi-Van's voice but Phi-Van had never said such a thing.

She was shaken. Truly Phi-Van had never said such a thing. A small horror opened up within her and spread. Lian realised for the first time that everything awful and fearful that passed through her or lodged in her was cast in her mother's voice in the theatre of her heart.

Her mother's voice ticked on distantly within her; a small, reassuring mechanism had lost its charm and become sinister, a marching toy grinning fixedly as it crosses a bombed-out street in a war zone. Lian was bereft and left frail as it marched away.

Phi-Van, Fi Fo Fi Mum had played a big part in keeping Lian strong.

The Language School had filled with American students. They were loud, nervous, curious. All were men. The military boys had to sneak away to meet Yemenis, since they were forbidden from socialising with the natives. The smallest encounters they had, at the *Aseer* stall, or an invitation to a qat chew, were seen to be exciting overtures, practised seductions by an enemy who had fine manners and ulterior motives. The *Aseer* youth, the street perfumers, the cripples and aged young had designs on their American identities. Lian almost envied the American students' cultural assurance. Being here seemed to strengthen rather than erode their beliefs and impressions. They saw what they expected to see and they pronounced their judgements with the assurance of the unassailable.

Each had an arsenal of true stories that, as a selection, gave a picture of Yemeni culture and people as the incarnation of cruelty, bigotry, misogyny. Some students, as soon as they realised that the world they had entered did not fit the selections they had read, reacted in fear. They began the inexhaustible, circular and always reassuring search for the mean and nasty. Some made a career of it and went back to lecture in America as scholars of the Yemen and its Islam-cankered primitives.

This place and these people could not seduce them, violate them or enrich them.

The exceptions were equally intense and passionate about their conversion. With janissary fervour they defended everything, separating Yemen from the human as absolutely as their virginal friends.

One young student from Utah, Andy, was an exception to both and his compatriots hated him for it. Andy's dream was to be kidnapped by Bedouin. Through him they could extract hospitals and schools from their embarrassed government and, according to all the tribes-men Lian and Andy knew, he would learn the essentials in return: riding, soccer and recitation. It would be fantastic for his language skills. He went out into for-bidden zones every weekend. I am an American. I have

a lot to offer. Every Saturday she caught his eye. Still
here? Yes. Wryly. *Inshallah* next week. *Inshallah*.

They passed through an expanse in which jewels
lay scattered about like pebbles. Purple, green, blue
and pale pink in many shades. Abdallah could
barely believe his eyes. After a while, however,
it was too much for his eyes and they accepted
the jewels as worthless before his mind could.
   They came to a vast city and entered through
gates built entirely of emeralds and having only an
ornamental purpose, as the city was usually
entered from above. The streets were deep ravines
and the doors of the houses were like jewelled
brooches set into the cliff face. All around schools
of glow fish, fed as pets, kept the city illuminated
in an eerie light, glimmering from around corners
and in crevasses. The whole city was embedded but
viewed from above glittered and glinted over a
great area, dazzling the mind and sight. Abdallah
of the Land thought this must be the capital but
his friend laughed and told him this was only a
provincial city, one of ten, and that the capital
was built above and below and was the centre
of the provinces. Abdallah of the Land was filled
with a strange hopelessness and ennui.
   They entered an inn for the night. It was
pleasantly lit, despite being a cave. They were
served several kinds of fish. Abdallah looked at

them with distaste and watched as his friend began
eating them with relish, tearing the raw flesh from
the bones with his fine white teeth.

'What is wrong?' the Merman asked,
stopping in the middle of a mouthful and eyeing
Abdallah over a silver fish. 'You do eat fish,
O Fisherman?' and his eyes crinkled pleasantly as
he smiled.

'We cook the fish first,' he said uncomfortably.
'There is no fire under the ocean!'

He picked up a pilchard gingerly and bit into
it. It did taste good. It was crisp and clean and
fresh. He forgot his qualms quickly and even
wondered why he had never tried raw fish before.
It was refreshing and delicious.

'Tomorrow we will explore the city,' Abdallah
of the Sea said, 'and over the next few weeks I will
show you the dominions of this small kingdom.'

Abdallah of the Land thanked his gracious
friend with all his heart and went to sleep, his head
whirling with jewels and fishes and images and
vistas of ocean territories.

The fine, dry street dust brushed the hem of her black-
embroidered black *balto*. She walked briskly near to the
mudbrick wall. Her legs swung beneath the folds,
muscles tingling, yearning for some violent endless
exercise. The courage to do something outrageous had
been slowly building in her. Helena was shocked and

delighted when Lian suggested jogging, but refused to accompany her.

At 6.30 a.m. on a Friday, a little after the dawn prayer, Lian, dressed in a long shirt of Nev's and loose trackies, hauled on her Nikes and went for a run. Her brown hair was tied back, bouncing and shining like a horse's tail. Her blood surged and she swung her arms in arcs in the deserted street. The dogs, still awake, turned their heads to watch as she passed. She ran down the cobbled road to the Saila, and up through Tahrir Square, through the winding alley of the Bauniya and out past the Qa Square. There was no-one about and the air was crisp against her face. She ran down the middle of the long street leading from the Qa to the university, scuffing dust and rubbish, hearing her footfalls echo up against the walls and the blue metal doors of the closed shops. At the corners she caught the early sunlight, shocked dogs and glimpses of the bare mountain to her left.

She had thought she was fit but her breath laboured. For the first time in all these months, she realised how thin and rarefied the air was, how little of it there was for her lungs to purchase. Her chest ached. She began startling the occasional youth or elderly man at corners. She stopped enjoying herself, caught and pinned in their shocked eyes. The old men muttered and turned away, too shocked to have their eyes see more, to see the strangenesses of the modern world. The young men stared, some grinned. Then, angling down a side street away from their eyes, she came upon a group of small boys playing soccer. They shrieked and laughed and, once her bobbing back and hair were to them, began pelting her with stones. Lian spun around and ran towards them, too tired to sprint, furious, her chest screaming with pain. She must have looked mad, for they paused only a moment and then scattered. She turned and loped home in the intensifying day, small stones rolling to her ankles and past her from the hidden stalkers.

She closed the door with relief and basked in Helena's amusement and celebration of the feat.

She didn't go jogging again.

'Pen! Pen! Money?'

Lian laughed. 'Story! Tell me a story! Any story! Koran story!'

As always, the children stopped and stared, blushed, twisted their toes in the dust, grinned and laughed, all their brash bravery wiped away in an instant. Mostly they ran away, reluctantly, tempted, but too shy to leave the groove of their practised lines. Story Lady, they called her, but until now had rarely told her any.

Asma was a black-eyed child with a peaked country-hood. She ran away, but inched back and caught up with Lian on the next corner, accosting her before she left her territory.

'Pen?' she said softly, a little uncertainly.

'A pen for a story.' Lian feigned boredom. Asma grinned. She grabbed Lian's hand and dragged her into a narrow alley, glancing back and forth to check for her competition. They sat together on a stone step and Asma looked Lian in the eyes in a long unsmiling stare, her mouth still, her pupils wide. Lian was momentarily disoriented and, just as she was starting to wonder what she might have done wrong or what the child might be expecting, Asma intoned in a deep, breathless voice,

'In the name of God the Compassionate, the Merciful. God alone is all knowing. And after. In the past once (God alone knows) there was a poor fisherman named Abdallah. He had ten children, the youngest born that very day ...'

The blue shadow of the afternoon closed over their heads as Asma rushed seamlessly through an action-packed version of the story. Lian's heart lurched with sudden delight. She watched the mobile face of her *rawiya* whose hands were swimming lightly through the air. The words were too rapid, too colloquial for her to hear more than the skeleton, but the hands spoke the rest. She could follow it as far as she also had read, and then the story became cloudy and dimmed with shadows she couldn't understand.

Ibrahim entered their strange, most suspect circle, their salon, their coterie. The literary boys of Sanaa (and in quite separate groups and separate occasions, the literary girls) had gravitated towards the tall crooked house near the Taj. Helena, Kobe and Lian presided. Everyone was witty, fell into the chasm in the language gap, to be rescued by Kobe's perfect grace and virtuoso linguistic skills.

Under the homely, familiar light of their *mafraj*, Lian was more at ease looking carefully and curiously at Ibrahim. He probably had short black hair but it was always covered. He had a moustache that grew naturally into the form of seabirds' wings. Lian knew that his eyes were black but they were still startling in the way that all black eyes are: they looked as though they were hawk-like pupils with no iris. The iris of his eyes could be seen as dim striations such as might be seen at the rim of an underwater volcano. After the dance, Lian was wary of him. His face and manner were gentle, soft-spoken and, if she shut out the sense that he was always absenting himself, his eyes were warm. The girls of Saba were famed for their wild beauty. Ibrahim was one of their sons but not a happy one.

Ibrahim hid his shyness and unfamiliarity with European women under perfect manners. Kobe met him with the equivalent and removed her *hijab*, revealing waves of sun-gold hair shimmering in ripples down to her waist. He actually blushed, much to Lian's amusement. Side by side he and Kobe resembled the stuff of fairy stories, the fine dark Prince and the fairy-fair Princess. Lian whispered to Helena, 'I'd give anything for a photo!'

Helena laughed.

As they ate, Ibrahim glanced at Kobe occasionally, one flick of the eye and then back to the group. Kobe was a beauty: oval face, clear skin, serene blue eyes; but she had a strange way of eating, fastidious to the extent that she appeared to be negating the fact that she was eating at all. Her hands moved with slow, fluid grace, noiselessly separating fragments of food with gentle but untender movements, raising them, inserting them without contact into a barely open mouth, shielded by her other hand. She did not appear to chew. Her hands tore bread with infinite gentleness, without a sound. Her fork neither touched her plate nor her teeth. There was something ghoul-like in her seemingly shamed complicity in the satisfaction of her appetite.

Ibrahim watched Lian and Helena eat simply and vigorously, laughing to each other, commenting on taste, on Yemeni bread, between eager, unconscious mouthfuls. He listened to their tales of bread buying and felt a little proud of women breadsellers. Kobe was utterly silent, deep in the processes of invisible mastication. When she finished she said, 'That was truly delicious.'

She looked unchanged. Lian and Helena relaxed

into the *mafraj*, their muffled bodies softer, satiety clear in their faces, their manner. Kobe had captivated him with her hair and lost him half an hour later with whatever lurked beneath it. He still found her ankles fascinating but it was fading.

He watched Lian without her being aware of it. Before the *tafrita*, before the dance, he had seen her a couple of times on the street. She had stood out. He had even once followed her, out of restlessness and curiosity, and because she was striding up the Sharia Jamal ahead of him and almost in the same direction. In her wake he picked up the titters and chatter. He had a memory of a long swinging step, faster than his own. A step, a blue *hijab*, an animal speed and ease, and her tallness. Chinese, he knew, from the words in her wake, but she was too tall. He had been startled when she glanced back suddenly, catching his eye but unseeing, as she crossed the road. She was suddenly clambering and gawky in her movements, then she settled into the strange stride again. Chinese; a fierce, black-eyed look, a face lit up. It was a moment until now forgotten but suddenly vivid. She was different and for a moment he felt afraid, for he saw her with unusual clarity. On the street he had recognised something. Now he saw a very tall, broad-shouldered, light-haired, gold-skinned Asian girl with a fierce and serious face, a painful look of constrained introspection, the look of a cripple confined in a beautiful body, and somehow she was familiar. He was afraid.

He looked down but could not stop his ears. Her voice was not that of a frail girl or of the girl he could see. It was rich, warm, amused. He heard a life in her voice and a low note of panic. He was afraid.

He turned to Helena and Kobe, to converse, to shut her out. Lian stood to get coffee and, as she moved past him, ducking her head to fit through the cupboard door that was the entrance to their *mafraj*, he smelt her. She smelt clean and salty. There was nothing sweet about her and he liked this more than he wanted to.

When he left after that first dinner, he was not clear-headed but he knew that he wanted Lian's friendship.

Ibrahim visited their household often, easing himself gently and courteously into a friendship with both Helena and Lian. He and Ammat al-Rahman met with them at the university and then he got Rahmana to visit the house with the more aloof Abha on different occasions. He offered to have his tribe kidnap them if ever they needed it. He talked warmly of his family and his plans to Lian, and, through him and Rahmana, Lian and Helena slipped into a different layer of Yemeni life and experience. Kobe moved out, having obtained an attachment to the Swiss consulate, warning them about tribal men.

Ibrahim grew up in a remote mountain village. He had begun to see it as remote, rather than the centre, long before his uncles guessed that he would leave for Sanaa, for school, then university. His father died when he was fifteen and his mother changed, becoming quiet and lemony, ruling the second wife with a hard voice, when before they had been friends. It was she who insisted that he get an education outside the village.

As a boy, he had a belief that he had too much blood. At fifteen he could feel the responsibilities of his life beating mercilessly in his chest, filling him. The fuller he got the greater his sense of emptiness and loss. He knew that he would grow up and dress well on Fridays. His father had been a just and honourable man and he was his father's son. He told Lian that the only reason young men and women were driven to admire the West and seek education was health. Lian didn't understand him at first. He meant it literally. The healing of illness, individual and community medicine, drove many he knew to Sanaa University and beyond. Engineers and doctors, they were part of the same project. But Ibrahim was too in awe of blood to become a doctor.

He could reason his defection almost in his father's terms.

He didn't tell her how imprisoned he felt in his family and in the face of their adoration for his father. His father had been good to him too. He remembered easy humour and an embracing love of children. He remembered stories. He remembered coveting his father's approval with pain in his chest. He had not wanted to live when his father died and he had had to

stand tall through the months that followed, whether
with the men who came to see them or alone with his
broken mother.

The two little boys dashed back and forth whooping and
shrieking with laughter. They darted in at Sheikh
Ibrahim, yipping, jumping and then standing still. His
wiry brown hand shot out and, unerring as a hawk,
nipped their penises:
    this one
    that one
    and there, it was back under the folds of his cloak.
They raced off again shrieking with laughter. His face
softened. His fourteen-year-old son watched him and
wished for his boyhood back.

A trick of the eye, a chance of nature from the start. He
was a passer-by, travelling in the opposite direction, but
even she could see that he was her double, a misplaced
man, losing name and family, looking to the outside for
something to shake him to pieces and see where he fell.
    Where this arrow falls make my city. Where this arrow
falls make my grave.
    She found herself in a fickle freak current, deadly
but surely transient, a trick of the light, of the strange

place, of circumstance. She hoped to wait it out, to swim with steady strokes, deliberately controlling her frightened breathing, and angle across it until its haul on her limbs and breath weakened and it left her, passing on to drag someone else away. Her heart lurched in his company, dragged out of her body. They became friends.

'When I was thirteen my father gave me a boat. With an outboard motor.'

He looked at her in astonishment and then laughed.

'Did you use it?'

'Of course.'

He looked at her with mock gravity.

'In the old times a mariner could not testify in court. His trade proved he was not of right mind.'

'In that case all Australians are mad.'

'Definitely, although you are only half mad, because you are a woman.'

She laughed and punched him. He looked startled, and then grinned.

'Domestic violence. An Australian custom.'

'Australia's not that bad. It's a lot like Yemen.' *What a lie*, she thought, as soon as she had said it.

'Let's go to the Tihama and find a beach and go swimming!'

'I cannot swim,' he said simply.

Lian looked at him with her mouth open for a moment, feeling her gills widen. Then she laughed out loud.

'I told you the sea's only for mad people.'

'You *have* to be able to swim! We can go down and just try it.'

'Will you rescue me from drowning?' He looked her up and down disparagingly.

'Of course,' she said. 'Don't underestimate us fisherfolk.'

At the Language School she heard herself speaking in a broad and earthy accent. She listened as she narrated wood chopping and horsey stories. She saw herself become the demo Australian. Quaint, experienced, rough and practical. Opinionated. She was only like this when speaking with the British students. Something in their clipped hedgerow voices brought it out in her. She noticed the desire to shock, to be the uncouth antipodean she thought they might expect. To make them think women were bigger and better and tougher down there. She was tired of the surprise they showed when she said she was Australian.

She felt herself taking on an identity dependent entirely on who she was with. She was losing hold of something she could not define, but felt a seeping away and self-disgust rising.

The language of God was driving her crazy. It was impossible to learn and the effort was changing her. Could a language take all that and in the end give only a travesty of communication? It was a kind of self-mutilation to learn it, a self-crippling, a self-destroying nonsense. A prison willingly entered, a mouth willingly gagged, a self willingly beaten unrecognisable. Already she had lost her family. They knew, even if they didn't have to hear her speak, that something she had done to herself had removed her from connection with them. Nev sounded sad on the phone. His voice had the calming tones he used to horses or dogs that had to be shot. Phi-Van was high-pitched, frightened, always rushing to hang up because of the cost. Overseas. Phi-Van couldn't even say the word without a high diphthong plea pressed through the second syllable.

Sometimes the thought of Phi-Van hearing her speak to street vendors, to breadsellers, to street children made Lian smile. She would have loved to alienate and impress her mother. But lately, the thought simply made her lonely and hollow.

Abha had just finished her final exams and was unusually talkative. But Abha was never comfortable company. She was tense, always too serious. Today she was slightly manic, charged with a euphoria and despair that completing her degree had engendered. Lian served the two sisters sweet red tea and sat without relaxing, feeling slightly guilty that she preferred the easier traditional Rahmana over the striking and unhappy older sister, her first Yemeniya friend. Lian saw Rahmana and Ibrahim far more often than Abha, who always waited for Lian to make the first move.

Rahmana was quiet, glancing sideways in concern at Abha. Abha was raving, staring at the opaque window, the closed door, occasionally at Lian.

'*Inshallah*, in a few months. I'll put in the application tomorrow! But I don't know how I'll leave this place. I love it and hate it, hate it, hate it!'

Lian murmured uncomfortably. She was in a phase of total love for Sanaa and all its inhabitants and, loyal in her passion, did not want to hear words against it.

'You understand, don't you? The more education we have, the less likely it is ... There is no hope for me here. What is this body?' She ran her hands over her breasts to her groin. 'Old!' She held up her beautiful arms and shook her hands above her head in a strangely parodic gesture. '*Men* have a life of the body!' She stood up and paced then stopped in front of Lian.

'I'll never have a child,' she whispered and Lian realised that Rahmana next to her was weeping. Lian had a sense that she had misunderstood some crucial, unspoken word. Abha's eye was accusing and Lian was disoriented.

'You might, in America,' Lian stuttered, insincerely, suddenly convinced herself that Abha would always be this exquisite, raging virgin.

'Marry! Abha, you must marry!' Rahmana cried, gripping Lian's hand in collusion. 'They all want her, Liana, but are afraid of her.'

Abha laughed, reached down and kissed her sister.

'What use is a fearful man who has power over me, Oh Rahmana?'

'You live away from your family?'

Ammat al-Rahman was too polite to sound aghast but Lian knew by now that this was a frightening, even appalling, proposition. Rahmana was just a few months married and lived with her husband's parents, for her husband Salih was in Germany studying for his PhD, and she was pregnant.

'There's only three of us: me, Nev and Phi-Van, my father and mother. My uncle lives on our family farm about half an hour away.'

'On an island!'

'Rahmana, you would like the Island. Apart from being flat and grassy and surrounded by the sea, and people wearing shorts and shirts,' she gestured with a palm chop at her thighs and shoulders, 'it's just like Yemen.'

They both laughed.

'I go shopping with my mother,' Lian said, thoughtfully.

'Oh, so do I!' Rahmana was delighted.

Lian smiled but her mind was suddenly on Phi-Van. Living in Adelaide and seeing Nev and Phi-Van rarely, Lian had discovered some things that she had always known but never considered. Phi-Van had excellent taste in fashion. She could not remember how it had been set up but periodically Phi-Van would come over for a day or two, stay in a hotel with Nev, and take Lian shopping. It must have been hard for Nev to support but he supplied Phi-Van with a credit card for the purpose. Phi-Van, looking beautiful and not much older than her tall daughter, would stroll proudly down the streets of Glenelg or North Adelaide, arm crooked in arm; and Lian, well, for her part, she let herself be led and guided. This unspoken giving on each part had boundaries that each respected scrupulously. In giving herself over to Phi-Van's whims, Lian earned in return Phi-Van's consideration of her personal likes and dislikes. They talked only of fabrics, colours and styles. Phi-Van took pleasure in dressing her daughter's body in beautiful linens and silks. She suppressed her own love of lace and became an artist in fine lines and contours. She played with her daughter's long legs, broad shoulders, muscular arms and sinuous rib cage. She made Lian's high breasts shimmer on an elegant stalk. She tried to choose things that reflected, in some subtle way, the sea; and she tried to have Lian notice her deliberation. She patted Lian, chatted in serious, analytical tones about Thai silk and the pretensions of a particular shop. She said *haute couture*, and *à la mode*, and *au revoir* to a French shop assistant. And when Lian giggled, Phi-Van smiled. She wrapped and wound Lian in a multitude of beautiful things and always, at the end of the day, they bought something which they both loved but which, in all likelihood, Lian would never wear. It was always too fine, too beautiful; and it was the buying of it that mattered. Lian had an extraordinary wardrobe, filled with these gifts. On the rare occasions when Phi-Van visited the flat, she would go to the wardrobe and, with a gentle faraway expression, stroke and finger the fabrics.

Under the terms of this strange truce in the war on Lian's body, Phi-Van wrapped her daughter in silk waters of her own choosing and was loving.

Phi-Van always returned from these outings exhausted. 'What have you *done* to her?' Nev would ask Lian, his voice leaping with happiness and undisguised satisfaction.

Lian had two of these gifts with her in Yemen. They hung shimmering in her wardrobe. Sometimes she spread them on the bed just for the shine of somewhere else to glimmer in her room.

Sirena stood out quivering and enraged on her high turrets. Her uncovered blonde hair and her jeans on a too-thin body caught Lian's eye. These once ordinary clothes now seemed a novelty. Sirena was shouting, tears of frustration and anger running down her cheeks.

'*Die Umweltsverschmutzung!*'

Fires ringed the city, as they had in the long-distant past. Black smoke rose into the clear evening air from the piled tyres which were used to fuel them.

The plump wife of the German consul eyed Lian with disgust and turned back to the visiting Danish scholars and American dignitaries. The art exhibition was becoming increasingly uncomfortable.

'These beautiful houses are simply destroyed by the Yemenis. They are like destructive children. They don't know how to value them or look after them. Only the Germans restore them like this, recapture their former glory. And we are not ever allowed to own them!'

It was a common complaint. Yemeni law prohibited foreigners from acquiring bits of Yemen.

'Don't talk to me about primitive. None of your idealism, your men-are-all-equal means jackshit here. You don't know the meaning of primitive until you have lived twelve years in this country. You should see their zoo!'

Lian turned away. She did not want to hear about the zoo. She was sure it was horrible. For this American to be drooling over its horrors, enumerating them as evidence, seemed unbearable. She shuddered.

'It's Islam. I can't work out if they lost their brains first or if the religion did it for them.'

Nightmare threads threshed in the storm at the fringes of both worlds. She didn't care. She didn't care what effort it cost her to keep hovering here. When she looked squarely at Sanaa and at the men and women around her, she thought she was looking at the city of God. She thought she could hear singing. She thought she could see her own reflection, peering at her from a darkened corner, running but waiting too for her to chase it.

She might never allow herself to tell someone that Ibrahim was a beautiful man. She would never be able to explain that he was and was not her lover. Perhaps she would have told Phi-Van, but only if they were face to face, shopping together as though shopping was just the tip of an ice-solid relationship.

The first time Ibrahim touched her skin, she froze, fighting to hide from him the tide of revulsion she felt towards him. She felt as though her body was suffused with a sudden evil ink bringing with it a memory of waking in the dark to the murmuring of Vietnamese. A small, diagnostic hand feeling her flat chest and button nipples under her pyjamas, impersonal, unaffectionate. And yet her body clamoured for more, for more of

Ibrahim and Phi-Van together, and she felt revolted, wild and reckless. 'Oh!' Ibrahim said and brushed the back of his hand against her blushing cheek and neck. 'Even your ears are red!'

Ibrahim raised his hand and held it touching yet hovering over her breast. It settled with a sensory pressure that rang through her spine and down. She blushed, unsure of herself.

'Would you do that if I was a Yemeniya?'

The hand left her body and rested inert on the red carpet. She almost reached out for it. He looked at her. She couldn't tell whether he was affronted or amused. But he was neither. He laid his cheek against hers, brushing it upwards, catching her velvet skin in his straight beard.

'I love you. I do not love any Yemeniya today!'

She tried not to think about what he had said. Her mind went scared and blank for a moment. She was glad he had misunderstood her. She hoped he had mis-understood her.

She decided that it would be safest to stop him from touching her breast. Perhaps that was what he expected.

Every time they were together in the *mafraj* after that his hand alighted on her breast and stayed. His eyes met hers, asking, not challenging, and she said nothing. Sometimes she even felt nothing. He might have been touching someone else's body. She almost despised him for thinking that he was with her.

Ibrahim lay on the *mafraj* diwan staring upwards,

one hand on her belly and the other around her shoulders. She thought they must look like diffident Indian lovers in Kama Sutra miniatures. She felt very detached, exhausted by the remote camera angle her mind gave of herself.

'We are still too interesting to each other. We won't know each other until our lives seem mundane. This being Yemen, that means marriage.'

She ignored the second half.

'How can my life ever seem mundane if you never see Australia?'

'Ya Ustraliya — oceans, parrots, bushfires, desert, funny English — you see, it's nearly mundane already.'

She laughed and, hiding her discomfort, began teasing him.

'If you were Australian you wouldn't be interesting.'

'If I was Australian I would cross the land barefoot singing the Camel Dreaming and I would speak twenty-seven languages, none of them funny English.'

She laughed, inwardly shaken.

'I take it back. You would be interesting. What have you been reading?'

'Bruce Chatwin,' he said, as if opening the door to a surprise party. 'I have a cousin who is friends with the Australian in Ibb and she gave it to him to give to me. Her brother in Coonabarabran sent it to her.' He paraded the strange words out with a flourish — *guess what I've got in my brain.*

The words sounded odd on his lips. She was uneasy

hearing them. Coonabarabran sounded as if it must be part of Yemen. She could not imagine him reading Chatwin or saying 'Gold Coast'.

'I don't have many feelings — I don't experience much directly,' she said, slowly. A wave of terror swept through her and the rushing roar of a storm rang in her ears. Something electric hissed in her heart. She could not hear what he said and just stared at him until the surge passed. She could not speak.

Phi-Van's voice whispered sibilant sick nothings in her ear at night.

A letter came from Phi-Van, disembodied, strange with venom. Lian's fingers slid over the paper nervously, making a skittering sound as she read. The letter writhed from subject to subject. It had no restraint and no sense of the Phi-Van Lian knew. It was the first in a series of letters that left Lian shaken, angry and, finally, resolved. She cut all contact and stopped writing home. Strangely, this made Phi-Van all the more present to her and the letters stayed with her in key phrases which could be charms to liberate her. They were proof that she needed to be free of her mother. They were proof of the savagery, appetite, relentlessness of Phi-Van's desire. They could, if ever needed, be shown to someone, at a strategic, intimate moment of confessions, explanations and tears. They would elicit support and sympathy from anyone who didn't know Phi-Van. *Ugliness, barren. Your sick love for your father. I am so glad you are gone. Never come back — he is happy now.* She saved them up to show Ibrahim as explanation, when the time came.

She knew but would not face that it was not what the letters said that mattered but how Phi-Van was feeling to have said such things. She could not admit to herself that all was not well at home. *Selfish slut. Pride, dishonesty, worm. Cold, a grey lizard, tearless. You are the onlooker, unlovable unloving unloved. Your voice will bring you sex but you kill all love. Give-nothing-take-nothing-LIAN.*

The carcasses were strung on the raised wheel. The headless necks trailed the sodden ground. Ibrahim's uncles moved methodically and efficiently, serious and practised. Only Ammu Mohammad smiled, chattered and joked, waving entrails in his direction. But he could see that this was because Mohammad was hating it and was acutely embarrassed at the small witness. Ibrahim tried to keep his face calm and serious in order to comfort Ammu. The sight was solemn and extreme. The blood and the irreparable nature of death struck him deeply. It was an event, though, not an absence, not a nothing. It was terrible, important and exciting. He once looked through a jagged hole in a wooden gate to a garden in Rawda and saw a naked woman, drying her long black hair under an apricot tree. He had been struck then too with this sensation. He had quickly looked away, out of respect for her and for decency, and out of shame that he had put his eye to a hole that should not have been there, but also because his excitement was too great to be contained. He almost thought he understood something. This was the opposite, but it was also beyond the ordinary day, out of time. It was also God. This time he looked steadily, unflinchingly. The moment of death. A woman in a moment framed by the withdrawn glance and the jagged wooden hole. The creatures' eyes turned inward and quiet when they died and the excessive red which they had always carried hidden or controlled rushed out freely and marked everything and everyone. Even his *kamis* was speckled, he was not sure how. He watched because his father had said that he should.

His uncles worked quickly and harmoniously around the yawning forms of strung flesh. All were marked and stained red.

The secrets of life departed and the food for the Eid was laid out and carried away.

He looked down at his feet. He slipped one out of his sandal and placed it over a large stone and pressed down until it hurt. His foot, hunched uncomfortably over the rock, looked like a small hen whose chickens have grown too big for her.

He was tall for his age, thoughtful for his age.

He turned to her suddenly. She could see only his eyes; a deep shadow fell across his lips.

'That is why the poets write. It's the same thing. They cannot experience anything whole.'

She smiled stiffly, trying to pretend she didn't know what he was talking about. He looked at her, silently, chewing his food. She was here now, he thought, but always half leaving.

'You are able to change. That's a gift from Allah.'

'That's a terrible curse. And keep Allah out of it.'

Her eyes were wild and he was delighted.

He reminded her then of Nev and she almost hated him.

He was looking at her with a strange expression. She wanted to know what he was thinking.

'What are you afraid of?' she asked.

'You. I don't know you. I only know who you are being now.'

She looked at him. It was fear, then. Why was he here?

He's slumming, Phi-Van said.

'Why are you with me, Ibrahim?'

'Do you have a problem with the me and you, or

with the Yemeni and the Australian?' There was
something hard in his voice.

She didn't answer, struggling. But she could not let
it go. Phi-Van was twisting her lips like this, eking her
voice out, doling out these words. She had a sense of
herself as lurking, as deceiving; hidden inside her
mother, interrogated as she was interrogating.

'I'm not a virgin,' she said suddenly, although
she was.

He blushed, looking down.

'Neither am I.'

The colours from the glass panes danced around the
high room. She watched a blue glimmer shift from his
lower lip to his cheekbone. She was shocked into
humility, and back into her own skin. A red light ran up
his face as he moved his face awkwardly away from her.
She reached out her hand and touched the blue mark on
his cheek. The red shot up her arm and fell off the edge.
He placed his hand over hers and then they ate in silence.

Lian fought against her friendship with Ibrahim,
using introspection, self-loathing and self-analysis,
using Phi-Van and duplicity, using her ability to be aloof
and hateful, but nothing succeeded. Her life drifted into
a dark phase of cavernous and insatiable need.

Ibrahim had served his mother's grief, becoming
a silent and self-negating perfect son. He let his

mother marry him to a girl of sixteen, placidly, almost absently becoming a husband, an unloving if hungry lover, and divorcing her, two years later, also at his mother's insistence. He sent her off with exemplary generosity, saw her freed by her barrenness from both him and her dreams, and then lost contact with her altogether. He did not think about this whole episode in his life much but felt a vague, irritant shame if he did. He rarely spoke of it. He pursued his studies with an energy he had never felt in his marriage, dreaming of escape from the selfless and absent boy he had been.

The night he told Lian all this, he felt clear-hearted. He stated in simple, brutal words, in English, the simple facts of his life and felt his relief surge in his temples and belly. Lian listened with her usual manner, silent and absorbed, as if nothing disturbing was being narrated, and he felt vaguely reassured, as if her silence erased the faint colours that always seeped into him when he thought or spoke of this story. But then she asked, 'What was her name?' and suddenly he was deeply, bitterly ashamed. There was nothing faint or fleeting about this shame, no easily evaded colour. This was a rush of blood in his marrow and, in his sudden bewildered misery, *he could not remember*. He was speechless, somehow disconnected from his own memory and visions. He had slipped away from it for so long that his own existence, trailing behind him, was fading, irretrievable. He stared at her, white-faced, and then leapt up, scrabbling for his *jambiya* belt and coat. He couldn't say the words *I can't remember* but it was a lie to leave. He just stood in the middle of the *mafraj* and then sat down again.

'Latifa,' he whispered, his mouth forming the syllables for him. Lian was looking frightened, drawn tightly into her *balto,* and he wanted to say something more. He wished he had said nothing. Latifa was beautiful. His sisters told him, for they went to the bath together. But Latifa never let him see her naked. She managed to give everything and give nothing and this shamed him the most.

'Does her story eat at you?' Lian asked finally. He looked at her slightly flinching face and the heat of his shame faded. He wanted to weep with relief.

She saw Ibrahim in the crowd. His stride was unmistakable. He swept towards her and she felt her face light up and then slowly freeze over as he ignored her, passed by and was gone.

'I don't want to see you any more.' Her voice was quiet and calm, as cold as Phi-Van's. She stood at the door, holding it as a barrier.

'Why not?' he looked stunned, then angry.

'Why did you ignore me today on the street?' There seemed no point asking anything.

He stared.

'I was treating you with respect! Other men were looking and looking. I wanted to shame them with the respect I was extending towards you. How would it be if I stared and smiled, or stopped and said hello?'

It was a private pleasure to Ibrahim to conduct himself towards her as if she were a Yemeniya, to elevate her in public.

'Does it matter so much what the people think, that you have to pretend not to see me for their sake?'

'It's for your sake, for your honour. Don't be a donkey!'

He was furious.

She turned on him and yelled in Arabic, '*Ya Aibatak! Yakhrib Baytak!* Your Shamefulness! May God destroy your house! Don't criticise me for not understanding a stupidity I could not possibly guess!'

He grabbed her. They were both shaking with laughter at her Arabic rage. He reached for her but she still evaded him.

Over dinner he said, 'I will never ignore you again.'

'What about my honour?'

'I will tie a kangaroo to the tassel of my *mshadda*. Every time you see me on the street look at it and I too will look at it.'

The next time she saw him he had a clumsy gold amoeba stitched to the tassel.

She thought suddenly that she had no idea if she had gained or lost weight in the last three months. She stopped still in the street. That was incredible. She began walking quickly, heading for home. Her body had either severed itself from her or it had finally joined to her. She wasn't sure which.

She remembered looking in mirrors, making every inch of her body stand the test of being measured up against something. She remembered passing shop windows, inevitably checking to see how thin or how ugly she looked today. Her body had changed. She had no idea where exactly it was right now. Was there a small roll of fat above her hips along her back? Were there rolls of fat on her belly when she leaned forward? Were her thighs smooth or dimpled? Did her inner thighs flap loosely when she ran? She had no idea. Her body had lost its objective form. Why? Was this an effect of covered clothing? Of knowing that no-one was scrutinising you? Did all of that come from having lived in a society of roving eyes, one's own eyes and everyone else's? She wasn't sure. It struck her as amazing and frightening that body obsessiveness had sloughed off like a desiccated snake skin without her even noticing.

'Why don't you pressure me to adopt Islam?'

She said it as a throwaway but as soon as it was out her pulse raced and she felt sick. Ibrahim's face closed, impassive, protective. A long silence swept like a mean, gossiping wind between them. Ghost voices nipped at her ears.

'You cannot believe in me, let alone in God,' he said softly. She leapt upon the words, relieved.

'Oh, God! Surely God is easier to believe in than a man!'

He flushed, disconcerted.

She touched his face and said softly, 'You are different. You are not good at this macho thing.'

He was suddenly enraged.

'Lian, I don't like what you think of men and I don't want to squeeze what you think is my badness to fit into what you think is goodness.'

He was sweating, suddenly, with the urgency to leave. He walked out the low door without looking back, out of her air, down the endless winding stairs and into the night air of the street. He found himself weeping as he strode away. He felt as though she was binding his arms to his sides. A slow immobility had crept over his limbs in that room. He had felt the muscles in his thigh cramping, his jaw stiffening. How he hated her!

He strode towards the deep black shadows where the moon could not reach in the unlit city. He entered the blackness until the shadow closed finally over the silvered tips of his *mshadda* and then he was gone. He hugged the wall and the darkness like a cloak around him, buried away from the moon. Low voices greeted him to let him know where they were and that he was safe with them. He answered automatically, letting them know that he was a man, a Muslim, passing by just here, safe.

He remembered standing at that first killing. He went back, a few hours after everything was finished, and stood in the centre of the blood-soaked earth. He was sinking under exhaustion but he had to think about it and touch it. He squatted in the churned red earth, smelling the metallic, peppered mixture of the dry earth wetted and the blood spilled. It smelt like birth. It smelt like the room when his sister Rahmana was born. Harsh, raw, cause for joy. He touched the strange mud and thought of the animals, fading, dying, wilting into meat, and the blood touching everybody. His own blood would do exactly the same. Women bled to become women. He stood up in the centre of the circle, a small erect boy alone in a rocky highland world and thought *it is now that I have become a man.*

Every time he saw Lian he felt himself losing something. She bound him and bled him. To regain his health he had to drift away from strangers and into the quiet network of greetings in which he was known. A Muslim. A good man. Ibrahim, son of Ibrahim.

'It is now that I have become a man,' Ibrahim said in a soft voice, smiled into the darkness and turned back towards Lian's house.

Lian had knocked on a strange door without knowing clearly what she was asking for. The door was opened by a man who looked surprised to see her there, for he had opened it to flee the house. Over his shoulder she could see dancing. Over her shoulder he thought he could glimpse freedom. Then they looked at each other.

They were the disinherited.

The next few weeks passed in a kaleidoscopic whirl. Abdallah of the Land learned and saw much of the land and the people under the sea. They ate fish every day, for breakfast, lunch and dinner. The people of the sea were nearly all Muslim and lived in harmony with the few Christians and Jews amongst them. He learned of their criminal justice system one day when they swam past a city more regularly planned and orderly than others. He asked Abdallah of the Sea what city it was.

'That is the City of Exiled Women. Women who have committed crimes are banished to this city, and live out their time in the company of their own sex and telling sad stories.'

'What are their crimes?'

'They have turned against their own in one form or another,' the Merman said mildly.

Abdallah of the Land was silent. This definition and punishment struck him as infinitely preferable to the system on the land, and Abdallah of the Sea persuaded him that this was the correct application and interpretation of the Koran. There was also a

*City of Exiled Men. Criminals simply stepped out of
the dance of life.*

*Abdallah of the Land was often chastened by what
he saw, for it seemed to him that the society he was
looking at was in some ways more devout and
contented than his own.*

*Wherever they went the people stared at him
and rippled rumours of the Lacktail spread ahead
and behind.*

An American couple sat in the far end of the *mafraj*.
The man wore a *mshadda* as a scarf and was handsome
and golden. Lian got an impression of a serene blue-
eyed man with a firm handshake but missed his name
in the rapid round of introductions. Karen was leaning
against the bolster next to him, dressed in traditional
embroidered trousers, her bare soles black-red with
henna and her feet traced with henna floral designs.
Lian had reached the point of mistrusting any foreigner
with hennaed soles.

Karen was perhaps thirty and had a sweet smile.

'Where are you from, Lian?' she asked, as soon as
they were introduced. Lian sat next to her and briefly
explained her racial and cultural origins.

'Oh, mixed-race people are so *beautiful*, aren't they,
honey,' said Karen, turning to her husband.

'Yes, sweetie.'

Lian could not see him, for Karen had a lot of yellow
hair. She assumed he could not see her either.

Karen was warm and conversational, chatting, a little formally, about Yemen, the times she had lived and worked there, her love for the country and people, her favourite things: the bread, the textiles, the art of Fuad al-Futaih.

'I discovered him for America, you know. In my own small way. *So* many of my friends have bought prints.' She laughed. 'I drag Darren back every year, even if it's only for two weeks! I feel almost Yemeni, you know, close to them, in my heart.'

Karen sighed.

'Don't you feel it too, Lian?'

'Mmmm,' Lian said uncomfortably.

'You know, I think you do! As soon as I saw you, your face stood out to me. That is someone different, I told myself. Different.'

Lian had had enough and began thinking through ways to extricate herself: to get up and, as if at random, hook a detaining conversation with someone else in the gathering. But Karen suddenly grasped her arm, leaned in close and whispered something extraordinary.

'You know, we once nearly adopted a Yemeni baby.'

Lian turned, caught, almost shocked.

'How?'

'Oh, not easy. Not easy at all.' Karen shook her head slowly.

'I would not have thought you could! Who would offer a baby to adoption, let alone to an *ajnabiya*, an American?'

'Oh, that's where you're wrong. There're babies all

over the place. They wanted us to pay for it, you know. I was really obsessed with the idea. We were supposed to pay for the mother's medical expenses for the last three months, the caesarian section, and then this doctor was going to make a birth certificate saying the baby was mine, and then we would just walk into DC easy as pie, six weeks or so later. We had been here long enough for no-one to question it.'

'And the mother?'

'No-one the wiser. Her family was organising it. She was going to marry her cousin or someone a few months after.' Karen was silent for a moment. 'I even converted to Islam, you know. They asked for that, the family. I never met them and although we didn't go through with it, we never got our money back.'

'Why didn't you ...?'

'Oh, in the end Darren wouldn't lie to the authorities at home. At the last minute, he said he couldn't picture himself smuggling a baby through customs. Couldn't picture patting me and saying it was someone else's, God bless him.'

She smiled.

'But what happened to it? What happened to the mother?' Lian's voice rose a little. *What happened next? What could happen next? How could this story ever end?* Phi-Van rose in her throat and a pain tightened her chest.

Karen looked at her, suddenly thoughtful.

'You know, I don't know. The doctor probably organised something. He cared a lot about it all and was very upset. I didn't feel like contacting him again so I never found out. You know, I even felt guilty and had to see a shrink back home. But we didn't do anything wrong. We have our own children to think about now, so it's lucky really.'

Late in autumn Lian and Ibrahim, on a whim, drove for a day through the dinosaur-back ranges, through villages and cleft valleys, down to the Tihama and the Red Sea to swim. Ibrahim told stories of carrying calves and baby donkeys up the cliff faces to the sky villages, there to live out their lives, as the adults could never make it up or down.

On the hot humid plains they melted to the car seat, gasping for the ocean. Lian was veiled and sweating; Ibrahim almost panting. 'I am a mountain man,' he said. His *mshadda* took on a grimy appearance and he pulled his *kamis* up to his knees. The plains stretched out in a bare panorama of straw and poverty, lassitude and decay. The small towns simmered under buckled iron. They passed periodic signs on the road, rusted and pockmarked, lopsided and fallen, saying *Subhan Allah, Glory of God,* meaning *regard with wonder this beauty and grandeur.* Near Hodaida they passed a half-buried tank, gun to the sky, with a goat on top of it, lording it briefly over the flock in the shade. Near Hodaida airport lay serried ranks of rusted planes, some snapped like cigars.

Hodaida was upon them, too languid to announce itself. It was a browned, dusty port, flaking off the edge of the world. The sea was there, a firm line through it all, but the sense of city detritus spilled out to the horizon. Rusted hulks, deserted black-market liners, unregistered ships permanently out of fuel, broken-down tankers too dirty to scuttle, and the distant blue freighters that would be gone next morning, all dotted the Red Sea in disarray.

They left their stuff in a room not much bigger than a wardrobe in a holiday apartment block in Hodaida and headed into the desert to find the coast.

At the edge of town, tin sheds, lean-tos and concrete block servos gave way to a strange desert, its sand brown but almost lilac-tinted, flecked as far as the eye could reach with scattered red and white: rusted tins and white plastic rubbish snagged in thorns, on rocks, half buried and on the purple lee of every hillock. Larger pieces neared, became goats and sheep, and then vanished, receding back into the indiscriminate speckles.

Past the last highway checkpoint, at which Lian, silent and hidden in black, passed easily for a wife, the land shook off the detritus and scabs of the port and shimmered, stark in a violet haze, emphasised by the pressing bellies of heavy purple clouds and deflected sunlight. A great ragged stain of flamingoes flew low over the road ahead, a gash of hot pink against the strange earth and lowering sky.

Ibrahim was silent, hammered by the heat. Lian was sweating in rivers under the *litham* and she lifted its layers to let the breeze blow on her face. As her face appeared, he grinned at her.

Shockingly, the sea was there, as wild and beautiful and deserted as any isolated southern beach. There were no big breakers, just the calm, light toss of reef waters, as deep blue and green as childhood. Lian was disoriented from the start.

They stood on the shore. Ibrahim felt his sandals fill with sand and shell grit and walked towards the water to wash them out. He had been here last as a boy with his father. From the ruined, woven straw hut behind him he could almost hear faint chatter and smell smoke. This is the one, Baba, he said, hoping the words would make it true. *She's a stranger and does not know our ways* ... He turned away from the voice and Lian was barefoot next to him, the black *balto* falling as if in slow motion onto the sand behind her. She was dressed in just a white singlet and blue sarong and her face was lit with simple happiness. His breath caught in his throat, choking him. Her fine arms. Her fine neck and collarbone. His blood pounded in his ears as her ardent, thoughtless nakedness burned him. He didn't want to look at her long in case she turned too and saw his dizziness and love, and the gift would be withdrawn. He closed his eyes and turned away to open them. He thought he could see his father striding up the beach in an old style sheikh's caftan, but he felt no shame. Her nakedness was given to him alone and he knew the apparition of his father could not see it.

She is a stranger and does not know our ways, so be generous and gentle with her, my son.

They splashed in the shallows, laughing. He saw her exultant, saw her speed and grace in the water as something mysterious, a power, marking her difference. She was a creature of the sea, from under the sea, as different from him as it was possible to be. She laughed in that heady, rich voice, dived and reappeared, slick and shining. Water ran in shining droplets down her neck and under the singlet between her breasts. Her arms were glistening. His heart was breaking. He played clumsily, holding his shirt bunched up in one hand, longing for something that would bring her closer but unsure what he would do if he could touch or, even for a moment, hold her. Out on the reef, beyond the shallows where he stood and waited, she dived and bought up for him living whelks and sea anemones which closed too rapidly and looked like red jellies on rocks, and told him of the stingrays fleeing just metres from his feet, beige with iridescent blue spots; and of the tiny fish surrounding her like flower petals. He told her that Yemen's main export was saltwater aquarium fish and she told him that dugong must graze here, as the acres of seagrass were bitten off at two inches.

Three ships in lilac silhouette hung on the horizon. Two were always there, Ibrahim said. Abandoned. They'd sink one day.

Lian stood dripping in front of Ibrahim, reached up her shining arms, and, on the deserted beach, unwound and removed his *mshadda*. He stood still, all his dizziness, grief and joy focused suddenly in physical desire. He closed his eyes and ran shaking fingers through his hair, shook his head and laughed. His hair was several inches long, fine and shining black. Lian laughed too but was shaken. He seemed very young, a boy in a long shirt, naked. He looked quite different but for the first time familiar.

'Dive with me,' she said, but he shook his head, unable to speak.

She dived one last time on the ocean side of the reef. The late sun slanted into the water, making dull rays and shifting shadows on the darkening blue sand-hole beneath her. The water rippled along her skin and her lungs heated up, throbbing and aching. The water pressed against her ears painfully as she dived. Down near the eddying sand she opened her mouth and felt the salt water fill it to the back where the arch of her tongue blocked her throat. There was no further she could go. There was nowhere else to go. She felt her death there, sitting cold and calm and ready against the last wall of her body.

The western wave was aflame and Lian was dizzy as she watched the evening sun hover above the sea. Nothing had made her home seem more remote than this. With the faintly lilac sands behind her, the lurid green palms standing in clumps like gossips, the dunes hiding the kangaroo-red camels, all stretching out of sight behind her skull, the sea before her could have been her own at dawn. Almost. At her feet thousands of hermit crabs tracked strange scripts across the hot sand, making a tiny, ceaseless noise. The sun fell from the sky and sank in a flash of green.

That night, under the squeaking fan in a dusty holiday apartment, she was white and silent, breathing painfully in the thick humid air. The room was very small. Vestiges of other lives pressed around her. Someone's empty suitcase leaned against the tiny wardrobe. Someone's pink dress hung like an ugly rag in the bathroom, serving as a curtain for a remote window. Dust whispered in the corners and a hot Tihama wind blew sad voices up and down the empty street outside. Then the terrible pressure against her ribs and in her skull made her speak. She felt herself implode as the words fell from her like small, long-stored clumps of ambergris.

'When we are together I am not here.'

He was silent. Then his voice came, quietly:

'Should that make me jealous?'

'No. I am nowhere. Now I am lying with my back against the ceiling cataloguing the experience so I can feel it later.' She closed her eyes, surprised by slow tears slipping down her temples. She felt incoherence settle in the room between them, pressing against her temples, against the back of her throat. But he was not silent with it.

Her face was a pale profile in the darkened room.

'In Yemen or always?'

'Always, but in Yemen ... I remember things.' Phi-Van has always known and seen Lian, lying here in a dingy room. Lian holding this beautiful man with his dark eyes curved over her face, his naked hair and his body shining slightly in the shadowy air.

Ibrahim held her tightly. How could he know this woman? How could he comfort her? He wanted to tell her that he loved her and that she was beautiful but that seemed somehow to speak to the other on the ceiling. He had seen this phantom, looking at him through her eyes. He didn't know what to say and he was afraid. He wanted her to marry him. That was solid. He wanted to say something that had nothing to do with her body. He wanted to love her body while he said it. Something had driven her here, to Yemen, maybe to him. Nothing he could say could do more than make the onlooker sneer and whisper doubts into her ear. He was speechless, wondering how to address her in private without it hearing. Lian's eyes shone and her brow was smooth as bone and he wondered what he would see if he really looked. But when he kissed her, she moved and moaned faintly and the deadly look was gone.

He suddenly grabbed her hands, pinning them to the bed, and hauled himself up onto her body in one smooth movement. He made a second gawky clamber and landed chest to chest, laughing awkwardly. His hands burned against the naked skin at her waist and, in a movement both fluid and harsh, slid under her singlet to her breasts. Lian's breath came in gasps. She pulled the singlet away. Her belly spun like a boat jibing, catching the wind then heeling, its sails taut, the prow cutting deep. She wrapped her arms and legs around his smooth, hard body.

She was deeply surprised.

The Storm

Lian and Nev were far from shore when the wind picked up. They had cut the dive short, knowing that a squall was coming in. Two crays ticked and wheezed in the white vat, enough for Phi-Van, for all of them, if they made salad and spuds. The rich blue markings of the armoured animals were fading, and the carapaces became suffused with a dull purple. Nev and Lian glanced up at the sky. It had thickened to a heavy blue maroon, with an occasional ragged tear through to the sky, eyeholes of lurid and impossible brightness. As they looked up, the first wind licked them like a curling tongue, and their cheeks were slapped with great drops. The sea had been waiting, slicked down and glassy, all day. Suddenly shaken through with storm lust, it quivered and awoke. Nev caught Lian's eye and started the engine. *Anchor up and batten down.* She knew and was flying about, packing and stowing as the small craft plunged and veered.

Under stormlight, everything takes on a garish and unfamiliar aspect. The boat was stark and white, blue-white in the violet light. Its very crispness made it look small. Lian felt as if she was seeing herself and Nev and the craft from a distance, a speck in the waves, a feather in a whale's mouth. Tiny details stood out. The chrome cleats on the transom hatches shone richly, slippery with silver and purple and black, tiny reminders that lines could be held and tied off. Behind rose a huge green sea, spewing small slags of foaming lace. The cleats were framed for a moment in seething green as the stern slid down the wave and then they were drenched in a net of lace, the streaming hair of a wave which curled in slow motion and then broke transversely across Lian and the stern. The cleats disappeared and the boat laboured slowly out of the ocean, skewed sideways with the water running like a spillway from the starboard side. A cold fear spread over her. Small drops of sweat mixed with the salt water running down her face. *We will die, now. We are sinking, this minute, right now. This is how.* She felt as though she was floating and all sound was cut. Everything was silent and slow. The boat was half underwater, slowly, slowly rising, white as bone through the green. The cleats broke the surface, cresting like leaping pilchards, and then they shone solid again on the transom. Lian was vaguely aware of Nev's shoulders and elbows, working hard at the wheel, spinning this way and that as he tried to keep the prop from cutting foam, fighting to keep the prop hauling the small vessel through the huge muscle of each wave, trying to divide water with the prow at an angle that wouldn't flip them. The crest of the next wave was so sharp that the prop screamed in the air, and the wind tried to pick them up from the underbelly of the boat. But they slid sideways, dropping fifteen metres in seconds into the dark valley. The prop bit water and laboured again to face the next. Lian realised that she was bailing fiercely. She couldn't hear the bilge pump but hoped vaguely that it was working. The crays were sliding silently back and forth on the deck. For a moment she felt completely still, and watched her arms soundlessly spill water to leeward, and the crays, legs splayed, sliding. Her own legs were spread wide, each movement surfing the violence. Then the noise cut in and all she could hear was the scream of the wind and the swell and settle of the engine, as Nev cut and revved the throttle, angling, waiting and then gunning for each climb. She knew so well what he was doing that, without looking, she knew what he was seeing from the sound of the engine. She looked sternward and bailed, the engine's commentary giving her 360 degrees of vision. She adjusted without thinking for each wall of water and each nuance of rage facing her father.

The green sea turned all white, churned and torn, flattening slightly as the gale rose. Nev and Lian inched the boat towards the coast more by instinct than anything. They could see nothing and the compass was reeling and inarticulate. Each mountain was scaled as if it was the only one, or the last in the range. Each valley gave that tiny moment of respite and preparation, before the next breaking crest was at two o'clock to port and they ran slantways up towards the sky.

Lian lost all sense of time. She balanced and held on as the boat slid sickeningly, sluggishly into the closing embrace of each wave. All fear left her and she moved as if in a dream, her body bailing for her, slipping, sliding and righting itself independently from her. Her mind was alive in stillness, spinning away on a fixed axis somewhere else. A still point in the churning, a light as removed as the hidden sun, moon or stars. Suddenly she was thinking of Phi-Van and she met the image with the surprise that recognises something was expected. Of course, Phi-Van, you would be here, wouldn't you. Phi-Van looks up at her from an open boat in still, winking waters. She is scaling a fish and a rain of glittering scales flicks out silently and then slowly falls like peach blossom onto the water. The silent storm hugged Lian close and she clung to the rapidly fading image. As if through a magnifying glass in a storm of petals, she could just see Phi-Van, curled now like a pearly foetus in the bottom of a dhow.

A single scale hovered, leapt and dived before her eyes, shining through the mist and spray. She realised it was flying erratically and rapidly towards them, darting here and there, wheeling like a seagull; a something, shining, in the sky. Then, on the breast of a wave as they swept past it, she realised it was the breakwater beacon.

Phi-Van was so angry when they got back that they couldn't say much about the storm. Her face was sickly white and her lips blue. She was gasping for breath, slumped over the kitchen table, when they walked in. She stood up straight, eyes burning, gave Nev a look of utter contempt and left the room. Nev and Lian leaned exhausted against each other, stripping off their wet things in slow, fumbling movements. Nev caught Lian's eye, interrupting her sightless stare.

'She loves me!' he whispered, grinning. Lian giggled, disgusted.

'There's *crays*!' he shouted over his shoulder. A pot slammed in the kitchen.

The apartment whispered and leered at her from the moment she woke. The windows made mouths through torn curtains and the pink dress fluttered conspiratorially. The water gurgled down the filthy plughole. Lian began to shake and couldn't stop. Ibrahim found her bareheaded but clipping the *balto* in place with shaking fingers. He wrapped his arms tightly around her black-encased body, feeling for her shoulders and ribs and breasts with his hands.

'Oh Lian. I love you. I should have waited.'

And Lian despaired then, for he was apologising for her one free moment.

They climbed out of the heat-struck plains and into the cooler air of the mountains. Lian tried to speak of Phi-Van and shivered next to him. Ibrahim didn't know what to do. All he could see was her shining arms raised above him, her warm naked body in the dim light; and the blood on the sheet that morning. He felt elated and wanted to lift her with him, but she was becoming more leaden each minute. What did all this mean to her? His skin prickled. Surely not what it would mean to a Yemeniya. This terrible thought brought him, scalp crawling, back into the cabin of the 4WD with her. She had no women, he realised. No mother, no sisters and cousins. She had never had them and wouldn't know how to share her experiences. A heaviness settled on him and he didn't know what to say.

'Maybe you need your mother, Lian. Maybe you should go home for a while.'

Her shining arms; her blood on the sheet.

Lian felt the storm break in her heart, then. As if sucked through a dream tunnel into the waking world, she suddenly found herself utterly alone and drowning. The driver's seat, with Ibrahim in it, was impossibly remote. She could see his mouth moving but could hear nothing. She laughed, grimacing, shaking, as her heart beat in a rising wind of noise and fury.

'My mother!?' *She is the one devouring me.*

It was Phi-Van, not Ibrahim, who had leapt at her,

who had slept at the perimeter of her defences only to be the more ready. And it was Phi-Van, not Ibrahim, whom she was fighting, and, horror-struck, crying over.

Lian was enmeshed in a web of histories, thrashing hopelessly. Thinking that she was escaping her mother's story once and for all, she had entered a strange land, strange people, a new and forever crippling tongue, and disconnected herself from her family. She had felt brave and free, for a while, but her mother's story had cast its shadow far longer than her own and, without her knowing it, had chosen for her the path her feet would take. The path was luminous because her mother's story had made it so.

Perhaps it was clear from the beginning that Lian, in running, would have to follow. Perhaps it is clear that if you have no story of your own, you fall prey to others.

Lian reacted with a kind of marionette desperation. She moved three weeks after the Red Sea trip. She felt as if she were dying and the Taj house had become nightmarish in her mind. She felt as if all she could see were signs. The guts of a slaughtered goat lay in a twisted heap by the street wall near the Taj and set her blood pounding. Kobe no longer spoke with her. Helena's brash, motherly concern she could not bear. It made her ashamed that she had ever thought badly of Helena but it also made her feel small and solid and opaque. And Ibrahim. He had something to do with it but she could not have said what. She had become silent in his company after they returned from the Tihama, watching him falter in hers, screaming on the inside but unable to utter a word. The storm blasted and boiled in her ears and she could not hear or speak. She accepted the vague sense that he had deserted her, unquestioning. It was secondary, remote compared with the vortex looming large now in her eye and mind. She was close, so close to Phi-Van. She could hear the jingle of an Australian current affairs program.

She fled Ibrahim with jerky movements and unnamable terror.

Her third house was a little crooked oddity in the old Jewish quarter, smaller than her previous two houses but more spacious, since she lived in it alone. Alone, she hoped to recover some of her aloof security and sense of self. The house helped. It had a secretive yet self-assured air, and from the street always looked, if not sleepy, then at least introspective. Its carved door was made of a weathered and grained timber, worn smooth by many hands. It had a patina given by the polishing touch of centuries of hands returning home. It had old blue paint embedded in its crevices. The raised spearhead escutcheon around the keyhole was smooth, chipped at the bottom corner. Two mangy dogs, a yellow bitch and a half-grown pup with a withered leg, sun-soaked habitually in the dust by the doorstep.

Her house leaned against the house behind it, even fitted into it like a Chinese puzzle or a lopsided piece of joinery. Its off-perpendicular walls seemed to settle backwards slightly, slumped and tired. It had a distinct belly, perhaps from age rather than architecture. The interpenetrated houses of the quarter huddled blindly together, hugging each other, warding off erosion, trying to be blind to time. Her house was decrepit. It had coloured glass windows and dreamed quietly and introspectively of beauty and dissolution.

But a house could not stave off what was coming. She could hear the wet slap slap slap of Vietnam, the spaces and faces she had never let in.

She wandered through the days driven, mocked by the spangled sunlight, buried deep, walking through water. She woke up in despair, lifting her heavy limbs through the motions of dressing, shopping, studying. Every movement cost her. Every step hurt her somewhere in the back of her brain, jolting some profound lethargy with unwelcome reminders that she was alive and had to function. She could not bear people. She could not bear thinking about what they thought of her. Every step in the company of the Europeans was as if walking on knives. Small explosions in her mind flooded her face crimson. What did they really think of her? They despised her, hated her, were disgusted by her. She could not discard the *hijab* and *balto*, even for a European party. She could not bear the thought of the American ambassador's daughter and the German consul staring at her body with the curiosity of discovery, the fulfilment of their thwarted eyes.

She could not bear the company of Yemenis. What did they think of her? Was it really OK for her to wear a scarf over her head? Was it really honest for her to be mistaken for a Muslima by shopkeepers reassuring each other? She began to avoid the university, suspecting her friends of duplicity and worse.

She could not even weep. She lay at dusk on her bed staring upward, wide-eyed, waiting for sleep and nightmares to relieve her vigil. Why had Phi-Van tortured her? Why had Nev loved her? Their words had become as inconsequential as marks on the sand at low tide and she could no longer feel guilt. She read Phi-Van's letters again and could no longer see appetite and hatred in them. She could hear her mother screaming.

God loitered on everyone's lips. God was ubiquitous. It was shocking to think of a world in which he had to be sought out, dialled up in the hope of a private line. Here one didn't need to wonder about belief. People breathed it.

Inshallah she heard herself saying. *Al-Hamdu lillah. Mashallah. Inshallah* I will have children, next year maybe. *Inshallah.* Later she sat on the bed, dreamy and disjointed. Her knees relaxed, her heels resting on the irregular white floor, shiny gypsum or packed plaster. *It's not like that at all. Why did I feel sincere when I said that?* This was a slippery and strange world, not hers, not theirs. Something brought on by the enchantments and witchery of the language. The easy phrases of social intercourse resonated in her ears and fell off her tongue without conscious choice but they had changed her, were changing her still. If God wills it. Praise be to God. Oh what God wishes! She used to know that they meant no more than *Hopefully. Lucky! How gorgeous!* Now they seemed to mean that she was something or someone in a slippery realm.

She had loved speaking Arabic. She had loved being mistaken for someone who belonged. She had loved the increasingly natural sound of the syllables and phrases as she heard them roll off her tongue. But her Arabic, which just a few months ago had charmed her with its strengthening limbs as its clumsiness gave way to an awkward grace, filled her now with hatred, self-loathing and bitterness. Every imperfection, the very slowness of its movements, the deliberate cadences abraded her every time she opened her mouth. She read her difference in every word of praise she received for her lovely speech. Ammat al-Rahman laughed when Lian said this to her.

'You will not be able to learn Arabic to fluency without it bringing you to faith. Ibrahim says it is the ocean that connects us and God.'

She had never been so lonely in her life. How could one know someone, or be known, if every conversation was a trade in objects: beads for bones. Every conversation was about them and us, whether genial or aggressive. Her language had just led her to this, and she could feel herself turning away from language to hear the sibilant madness and the slap slap slap of her own silence.

'Oh, ya Liana, of course we watch our weight. The Yemeniya likes to be lean, *rashiqa*, elegant.'

'Oh, Rahmana, we don't all live unmarried. Most women marry.'

She turned away.

Nothing had cut her off more than being the outsider, looking in on a life that was as ordinary and as familiar to her as any life could be.

This place had drawn and repelled, had aroused desire and disgust. These were all refuges from the horror at the heart of it. All selves were provisional, forgotten in closets, hung up by pegs on a line to dry. And thinking thinking thinking was just a way to drown out what could be heard. She stepped over her two sleeping dogs, eyeing them warily, and cranked the lock of her crooked house. The dogs had opened their yellow eyes but didn't move. They had learned that she didn't kick.

Lian lay back on the bed, tears running down her temples and into the dusty *hijab* she had not yet removed. The multicoloured panes of the crooked windows fluttered on the age-polished white and yellow walls. The children shrieked outside.

She stared upward in her sepulchral room, trying to flick over external objects and trying to prevent the inward rolling eye. So beautiful, this nonspace, this impossible place. Why had she come here? She was finding only that she had never had anything other than this nothing.

Something murky cleared in Lian's vision and for a moment she thought she was inside Phi-Van's cupboard, one of the frozen talismanic fragments shoring up her mother's ruins.

Three big green leaves slap slap slap

She floated through the dusty streets. The connection with Australia rattled, dry and fragile. Australia was becoming rich in her dreams and too remote to be real in the remembered insect voices on the phone and the insect spoor on the page. She felt transparent and was grateful for her enveloping cloak.

Sanaa had become garish, populated with clowns, caricatures and an audience, anonymous and aware, just beyond reach. Eyes passed her in the street with the slightest flicker and she wondered who it was she had just met and whether or where they had met before. Everybody knew her. She was in centre stage and could see nothing.

The students themselves took on roles around her as outlandish as her own. Lynette played the crowd, waving back, shouting, American to the tips of her uncovered red hair.

'Aren't they *kind* really, don't you think?'

Her hungry eyes clung to Lian's face.

The crowd shouted that they loved her and she smiled, distracted.

Adrienne stared out of the window at Sanaa and her heart beat so heavily in her chest that they all heard it. Then it shook her, woke her in the night and sluiced the blood around her body at such speed that she fainted if she stood up. Crippled by waves of inexpressible terror she had to be taken to hospital and then sent home to Marseilles. She told Lian that Sanaa was the most horrible place she had ever seen, heard or smelt.

The European men twittered approvingly about the increasing number of uncovered faces, sure that there were more real women on the street now that they could see some. The American men compared beheadings they had seen in Saudi Arabia. Those without beheadings visited prisons and zoos in order to catch up in souvenir atrocities.

Three big green leaves slap slap slap against a broken bamboo pole

The dogs barked and whimpered and the cats howled through the night, their calls amplified in the thin air and by the high walls of the houses throwing them back and forth to hang like forgotten washing. The call to prayer wound itself up to pitch, sizzling for several minutes through the ancient broadcast machinery until it rang out crackling, silencing the animals in the predawn. *God is great and there is no other God*, in a voice ragged with static and microphone whinges.

And for all that the voice was beautiful.

When she passed through the donkey market it was deserted except for the maimed, retired donkeys, sleek and fat above their twisted or missing limbs.

She wondered if the sweet-faced and cheeky Yasmin had not cursed her.

The bougainvillea all over Sanaa flowered, hot as blood, bright as fire, trailing the stone or mud walls between the houses.

The body of a young girl was found in the metal rubbish crate at the end of her street.

Three big green leaves slap slap slap against a broken bamboo pole. Mei-Ling is face down on the roadside, naked, blue-white in stormlight, her long hair matted with purple.

Everywhere around her she saw mothers and daughters and saw what she was not. There was not much to see on the street unless you looked, and then it became frighteningly revealing: there was love, anger, control, comfort, bitterness, desire, and terror to be found in the glances of mothers. She could not bear it and could not stop. She wanted to know why and how the girl could have been so loved and killed too. She wanted to know the terrible stories but not as souvenirs. She wanted to know what had happened to her, Lian, when it seemed so damaging yet so minor by comparison.

She stopped attending classes but read the sea story and the Koran obsessively. Another letter came from Phi-Van, after a break in the deluge of letters of nearly a month. The writing was shaky on the envelope, but she didn't open it. The sea story was intensifying, pressured and frightening as she sank deeper into it looking for signs. She poked through its words and phrases for answers, more and more panicked as she neared the end.

Ramadan began in midwinter and she fasted, alone but in unison with everyone else. Her body and mind were starved to stillness. Ramadan, a brief, luminous month, bought her a strange peace. During Ramadan, the jolting intimacy with Phi-Van faded.

She lay on the settee in the rhomboid courtyard of her little house, staring up at the ever blue sky. The settee was placed so that the head end benefited from a rise in the floor. The stone-flagged floor had the undulations of some rolling meadow. The late yellowing sunlight slanted in, catching the white-plastered, round-shouldered forms of the high walls in white gold. She was most beautifully entombed in Yemen. She could feel a kind of death stealing upon her daily and wondered if she would soon not know how to live in her own skin. Her body had begun to seem much tougher and more enduring than her self. In front of her the shadowed wall was blue, the kind of blue you see on the shadow leeside of sand dunes. Spiralling in the sky innumerable small kites wheeled and played. They were not hunting. They were enjoying the thermals rising from the rustling, softly reeking city. She lay and watched this every evening, her empty stomach cleaving to her spine, weak and beyond active hunger. The birds of prey in the blue sky, the glittering expanse of bright gold darkening, receding, tracking up the wall, the loneliness, but most of all the airy arcs of the remote birds signalled a state of light-headed rapture and contemplation. She listened intently to every familiar moment of the advancing evening. The streets outside chattered and bustled as everyone rushed to buy the last necessities, samosas and dates, oranges and bread, to catch the market stalls before dusk, to beat the traffic home. The noise rattled upwards, crashed and rumbled and then evaporated away, dissipating like wood smoke in the clear air. As the sun left her high courtyard, at last the streets hushed. She knew that there would only be dogs and a few late stragglers out there. The dust would be settling noiselessly to rest. She thought of every soul in the city breathing with her, waiting, feeling the same stereoscopic connection, all hungry, all anticipating, all calm. Picking up the pulse, the muezzin began to chant. The air was filled with the insect sizzle of poorly amplified voices. The minarets competed from different angles in the running, modulating prayer before the call. The birds started to thin as the departing sun slowed their exciting rush of air. She imagined the sun heading inexorably down its path, tinting, tipping, slipping behind the mountain.

Then the rush: the loudspeaker is cranked up audibly. The sun is gone and the call rings out clear and vibrant, a spiralling warm wind, exciting. Her heart leapt up and she began to float with the winding, invigorating voice.

Allahu Akbar! Allahu Akbar!

She thinks of the city, rich and poor, men and women, children and the few foreigners who tap into the pulse of something simple. No-one goes hungry in Ramadan, that is what she has been told. She is willing to believe, wanting to believe in the harmony of shared experience without distinction. She feels that she is the invisible participant in a dance.

Hayya ila as-Salah!

She leaps up and floats to the kitchen and begins stuffing dates into her mouth.

Someone is playing 'Great Southern Land'. It floats on the air, out of the window of the French Embassy down to the Qa, swirling through the dust to Lian's keyhole. She turns the key in her heavy door, cranking the lock as silently as she can, ear straining for each thread. She opens the door onto the deserted street, bewildered and enchanted, dreaming but awake. The light of the day is passing through a rapid and luminous fade-out, and the streetscape looks fake, like a theatre or a special effect. The voice seeps into her ear like smoke into an empty house. She hears her own voice, shocked at how thin and unused it sounds, how strange the English syllables feel in the soft flesh room of her mouth. Then one of the dogs that lives on her doorstep catches her eye, raises his golden throat, closes his eyes and howls.

She realises that she understands dogs.

Once Lian was alone, hungry and contemplative enough, the sea story made its move. She turned one evening in the courtyard and was somehow unsurprised to find a giant fish in the shadows, moving languidly. *Assalaam Aleykum,* the fish said in a soft voice. *Waleykum as-Salaam!* she answered automatically. She made out the form of a greenish human being in the twilight. The fish had the head and torso of a man and the long tail of a fish. Her heart began to race and she quickly closed the door to keep him there.

And she was suddenly fine. She had Abdallah the Merman, with his decent, two-dimensional story face, leading her by the hand. Even when the sea was black as treacle and as difficult to move through, he was there, explaining the sights she couldn't see for her tears and suggesting he take her to the Queen of Sheba. He could talk under the sea but at first she could not. She had not the facility until he taught her. Abdallah the Merman had a good look in his eye. Honest and filled with undersea principles. Decent and upright and anything else she needed him to be. The streets no longer bothered her and the terrible dreams and visions left her. Of course she moved slowly: it was water. And the blue! The blue. *Subhan Allah*, she said and Abdallah the Merman flicked his coral Merman tail and smiled warmly in agreement.

Abdallah told her everything she needed to know and was wise to the ways of sea and land. Abdallah gave his friendship freely, warmly, but not crushingly. He understood when she said that Phi-Van's story had devoured her. He said that, as her friend, he would slay it and release her. She said let's drown it and me in it. He said if you wish.

And once when he asked her what her story was and she was silent, he said that some stories are hard to tell.

The days passed with Lian in a strange, self-absorbed, self-repelled dream. She walked through the city, disconnected but affected by small things, by minutiae. Against her remote madness, the brilliance of life played itself as if projected against a screen and she watched, sometimes caught in it with a lump in her throat, sometimes enmeshed in horror, and in rare moments weak with joy. It was winter in the city when it would have been summer on the Island. The figs and plums had been and gone in the barrows of the *souq*. In her room, the silk dresses were laid out on the mattress, and she was stabbed by the submarine glitter and the faint perfume of Phi-Van whenever she lay down on them. At night, Abdallah the Merman hung almost motionless in the current in her room, the blue dots along his tail picked out in the darkness with a phosphorescent glow.

She had not told Ibrahim where her new house was, and, although he found out almost straightaway, he waited, hoping that she would ask for him through Ammat al-Rahman. But, although Lian still drifted into the university occasionally, Rahmana was worried. Lian was cool and aloof, friendly but no longer like a friend. Ibrahim's chest hurt at the thought of what it might mean, afraid that her desertion was his fault and somehow sure that it wasn't. He waited, bewildered, tormented by the gift of her nakedness and the backward arch of her body in his arms, the skin from her thigh to her throat against his. He could not go to America, not now, even if the visa came through. He waited.

Lian began leaving the city in long wild treks, sometimes with Abdallah the Merman, sometimes alone. She took the story to read sometimes but began rereading what she already knew, afraid of what would happen under the sea if she read on.

She roamed through the mountains surrounding Sanaa, many of which were military zones, access prohibited. She would catch a taxi to the edge of the city and then walk, frightening the taxi driver with her unconcern and frightening villagers with her strange gait and Arabic, her self-containment and peculiar interests. She discovered a long dry watercourse which wound through sparsely vegetated hills and rocky escarpments on one of these expeditions. She scrambled along it, elated, scaring shepherds with her incongruity and determination. They kept their distance and she didn't see them. She felt alone and free. The creek bed curved and twisted, water having once gouged steep banks into the thorn and cactus lands, but water, so evident, was nonetheless imaginary. Broad pebble banks rimmed the edges of the bends and she could see in her mind's eye the eddy and stillness of the shallows at the rim of the rushing torrent. She clambered through the rocks slowly, as if waist deep against the current, singing under her breath. The stones were dry but faintly beautiful. Wet, they would have been red and green and gold. The watercourse narrowed and she headed higher into the hills, exhausted but still singing. She was alone but the air sang about her, and other voices joined her in her head.

She stopped still, looking back across the long, now indistinguishable wadi through which she had come. A violet mist hung over the hidden city. The mountains behind seemed to hang above the ground, faint gold, and, in the far distance, jagged grey blue. She held her breath but the world around her still sang. With her own crunching footfalls stilled, the world was filled with noises. Insects, sunlight, goats, distant shouts and shrieks of children; and, nearby, a voice, not her own, rose from somewhere but it could have been anywhere.

The land looked deserted but was inhabited by invisible beings. The singing voice rose and quavered, then hovered on the rising heat, singing of a broken heart with a light and almost joyous purity. More earthbound was the hidden sound of bleating and other more contented goat or sheep noises. The land was bare and dry and rocky, enduring a hard highland winter, and was otherwise featureless except for some scattered straggling thorn trees and the long runnels in the riven and torn earth. Lian struggled to pick out the words of the song but gave up when all she deciphered was *my broken heart*. The familiar dismay with her foster mother tongue threatened to rise but at that moment five white goats' heads appeared bobbing behind a nearby thorn bush. They clambered out of the earth, followed by seven more, all heading purposefully to her left. A girl's head then appeared from behind the thorn bush, rising from a dry riverbed hidden in the folds of earth and rock behind her. She seemed to be gliding for the light, wintry heat-shimmer wrapped her ankles. The girl's face was hidden behind a dark brown cloth with a glittering beaded edge, and under a wide-brimmed straw hat on her head which cast a dark shadow down to her breasts. A richly patterned red cape covered her shoulders and arms, held lightly at the front by a fine brown hand. Her skirt was of deep red woven wool striped with broad bands of silver. Her voice spiralled up and then stopped abrupt and alert, high in the sky, as she caught sight of Lian. The girl looked over her shoulder, then to Lian and called a greeting intended to float both ways. Her step was light. Lian answered just as the head of an old woman appeared from behind the thorn tree. The old woman also called a greeting, warmly, dismissively. She had a brown-skinned face, worn and fierce; hot black eyes. Her hair was covered by a black, red-edged scarf. Her clothing was also red. Her form was the exact shape and size as the girl's in front of her, but it was the face, visible and as attractive and elusive as the voice of the girl had been, that drew Lian's attention. The woman was just passing in the footsteps of the girl, a little way in front of Lian when she too cast her glance backwards, a rapid movement, like that of a bird checking its safety zone before relaxing its vigilance. A third head appeared from behind the thorn tree and a spry, ancient lady leapt up from the wadi. Her face too was uncovered, her hair bound in the old country style of winding a *hijab*. Her body was tiny and bent, a light caricature of the two in front of her. She was dressed in black and carried a long stick. She greeted Lian, and then herded the woman and the girl and the goats before her towards the mudbrick village camouflaged in the middle distance as a brown, churning wave crest in a sea of earth and rocks.

And then Abdallah was at her side, calming her rising panic and loneliness. It is the way of the people under the sea, he said. *Maybe the land too. But I have stepped out of the dance of life.* He gave her a serious look, a compassionate look, and stretched his fins. We'll swim, he said, changing the subject, and she headed down the wadi with him, relieved.

Three green leaves slap slapped against a bamboo pole. Mei-Ling lay on the roadside, naked, her long hair matted with purple.

It began to rain in heavy, smacking explosions, each splash so loud and particular, this upturned cart in the road was as big and as small as her earhole. The baby Phuoc was a neat, lifelike bundle in the gutter, still wearing his red tracksuit, his bottom up and his face sweet and unmarked, turned her way. She could feel the warmth of his body burning her ribs and the pain of his knees gripping her waist but he was not going to get up, raise his arms and settle against her hip again. The rain pelted his head deeper and deeper into the red mud, lifting a steady pan sizzle past his nostrils, spattering his eyelids, until his face disappeared. A kettle, a straw mat and a packet of cigarettes were at her

feet. She knew that if she walked around the cart, she would
not find her mother. She could hear her mother screaming
and then not screaming but that was not in this rain. She
stared down at her soaked pink dress. The churned earth at
her feet was leaking blood. Each rain drop smashed and
separated the clotted pools, and then the stained water
carried clumps of it away.

APCs were passing passing passing, leaving tyre tracks
in the strange-smelling mud. Sooner or later she knew one
would stop and terrible things would follow but she could not
flee. She squatted down next to Mei-Ling and stroked her
sister's leg.

Ramadan ended and Lian found herself alone. Abdallah
had sunk graciously back into the teeming world of
words and, for the first time in her whole life, Phi-Van
was absent. There was no sense of being watched in the
room. Lian felt almost too weak to move. She lay in utter
calm, the sum total of her self simply the vague flitting
images, random landscapes and seascapes, drifting
through her mind. She felt herself leaving, newly pure
and translucent, water.

Ibrahim saw Lian's sightless eyes and floating walk
on the street one day and was too shocked to wait any
longer. His anger and turmoil at her desertion melted
away. He slammed the knocker against the ancient door
and she opened, looking thin and light-hearted. She was

strung taut but joyous to see him. She seemed extraordinarily alive.

'How are you?' he asked awkwardly, his relief showing.

'Good!' she said, leaping up the stairs ahead of him, looking back, not asking him in, just assuming. He slipped in and closed the door. When he turned back to the darkened stair, she was gone but he could hear her rich voice calling down through the levels of the house, 'Ibrahim! Ibrahim!'

His happiness was a pain and a pressure in his blood and his step was light up the stair. Over dinner in the *mafraj* he noticed that her hair, which fell uncovered and shining over her shoulders, was longer and looked darker than in late autumn when he had last seen her uncovered. She was quiet but so changed. She had a solid, fine and glowing look which passed, fleetingly, back and forth in the room. He could say nothing and could not touch her but, as they ate together, he tore bread for her and watched as she accepted with no awkwardness and none of her former, odd consternation.

And so Lian resurfaced and slowly re-entered the world of people. There was the hint of spring in Yemen and early autumn on the Island. A ghost wind blew in her ears as she stared at the still azure skies above Sanaa, and ghost gold grasses swayed as she watched the vines greening in Rawda. The sea story was nearly finished and had lost its wonder and its terror. As she re-entered the world above the page, she emerged from a profound deafness. The streets were rich with, not the hum and indeterminate buzz of a life from which she was excluded, but with conversations, the ordinary sweet domestic exchanges of ordinary people; from which she was, nevertheless, excluded. She listened, charmed, the outsider, eavesdropper, the hidden lover. She listened, bereft; but calm with it.

'Why, why, did you buy chicken? I said *goat!*' The soft voice rolled over its rounded consonants, strangely clear from behind the black *litham*.

'Chicken is poor man's goat!'

'Mohammed said he would fix the car if you' ... 'Unbelievable! Impossible!' ... 'She did! I swear she looked and smiled!' ... 'Call this a shoe?'

'Lady of Stories!'

She heard it clearly, with no delay, no lightning riffle through the mental dictionary. She recognised herself in the call instantly, sifting it from all the other cries and calls of children, knowing that this was meant uniquely for her. She turned, as two filthy-faced girls ran towards her. Brash and laughing until a metre from her, then suddenly wavering; shy, voices quiet and eyes averted.

'We have a story for you!'

'Once upon a time there was a man who lived under the sea with his people, who also lived under the sea in beautiful cities, made of jewels. One day, as Abdallah the

Merman was swimming in the jewelled streets, his big toe caught in something, and he was suddenly pulled from the street, up through the water towards the sun. He found that he was caught in a fisherman's net and he thought to himself, this is God's will, so I'll see what happens. I have always been curious to speak with and get to know the men of the land, and sure there will be one at the other end of this net.'

Ibrahim had drawn her back into the world of his family, of Ammat al-Rahman, who was due to give birth, and of Abha, who was also headed for America. Lian found herself, if remote in feeling, wiser and more quietly sure than she had been. Life took on a strange, lurid calm in which she was charged and electric but almost at peace. She had almost no feelings at all and, if her fears of Ibrahim were gone, so was her passion, what there had been of it. It gave her pleasure to be in his company but she did not seek it out and her body was so absent that, instinctively aware, he didn't touch her.

Her disconnection, fretted at, analysed, packaged and unwrapped, denied and feared, had become itself. She was fully and completely disconnected and with this obvious, easy, latent state came also this peace. She felt pure at heart, as if she had welcomed a feared guest and found her benign, and her mind was clear. She thought of Phi-Van but only with a detached sadness, even warmth. She could not have said what it was that she understood but she had none of her former feelings for her mother, either.

Such peace cannot last.

Lian was not dead, and her clarity of mind and spirit was granted in part by exhaustion and the relief of surfacing, lungs intact, from a madness, which, no matter how gentle, had seemed the mirror image of drowning. The more her faculties and her body returned, the more confusing her returning chaotic feelings became. The days and nights lost their sempiternal faces and became individual: some happy for her, some despairing, some disturbing. As if falling from a redolent, vague and shining dream of unending stillness, Lian fell down, down, back into her body and into life in Sanaa.

She sat with Ammat al-Rahman, her cousin Ruqaya, grandmother Halima, aunt Asma and uncle's wives, Ammat al-Aziz and Asya, in the long *mafraj* of Ibrahim's family home, drawing on the *madaa* and talking. Women came and went, sitting for a while, conversing, drinking the too-sweet red tea, leaving again. The conversation floated back and forth, always swooping down from one side or the other on the differences in the lives of women in the cultures outside the walls; on the respective practicalities and difficulties of daily life; on the roles of men. How do you buy a bra, *here?* how do you buy a bra, *there?* The honour and weakness of men. Lian listened, her body curved in the folds of her cloak, her arm crooked over her raised knee. It was idle chatter in golden afternoon light but, despite the light, the clear voices and the sculptured beauty of the room and the dark and loving eyes of Rahmana, she knew that the person answering these simple curiosities in formal hybrid classical Arabic was not her.

And then, once when leaving Ammat al-Rahman and Ibrahim's family house, Rahmana leaning heavily into her arm, Mohammad, Ibrahim's oldest uncle, thrust the family Koran into her hands.

'Read! Read anything!'

Rahmana clutched her arm, eyes pleading. Lian took the heavy volume and opened it near the back, looking for the shorter verses she knew well. She read the Surat al-Layl in a deep rich voice, swelling with the waves of the verse, her fingers feeling the embossing of the ornate cover. She didn't falter, for she knew it by heart.

Ammu Mohammad took the volume back from her and murmured, 'Thank you!' catching her eye for a moment with a look almost of wonder.

Ammat al-Rahman walked with Lian out to the street gate, holding her hand in both of her own.

'O Liana! You really are one of us now!'

When Ammat al-Rahman gave birth to a son, Lian was invited to spend some time at the house. She was nervous, unsure suddenly if she was being honoured, if she could refuse, and, privately, if she could bear to be exposed for long hours to the faces and conversations of others.

As she entered the familiar house she instantly regretted having come. Despite the troubling relationship she had with this family, she was welcomed softly by Halima with gentle hands clasping hers and ushered upstairs to the *mafraj*, greeted warmly by everyone. The house was full of men and women but the *mafraj* was all women and Lian caught the eyes of Asya and Ruqaya with relief. Rahmana was in the cushions at the far end, pale but elated. She was surrounded by bunches of herbs. Lian kissed her and sat beside her. The baby was placed in Rahmana's arms and Lian smiled into her eyes, disoriented by the joy she saw there. Women bustled back and forth. Rahmana's mother and grandmother, mother-in-law, several aunts on both sides, and four sisters moved in and out, bringing giant straw mats, laying them on the floor and placing mountains of bread, *tannour* fish and salads for the meal.

The baby whimpered and smacked his lips stickily. Then he scrunched his face into a rigid frown and froze. Rahmana broke her conversation with Lian and stared down at him. For a moment she looked confused, then a ripple of the same frown washed over her face, then her eyes widened.

'Oh God!' she wailed, holding him up. Halima, sailing by, whisked him from her. In seconds, Asya, Halima and Rahmana's mother-in-law had him cleaned, changed, bundled and serene-faced back in his mother's arms. Rahmana moved her body painfully on the diwan and grinned at Lian. Lian grinned back but she was impressed.

Ibrahim's visa came through and, for the two weeks before he was due to leave for California, he spent most of his days with Lian in her small crooked house. They didn't talk about the future or the past because Lian silenced him when he tried with such terror in her face and voice that he was shocked into waiting. They ate together and talked of other things. He imagined luring her to America, returning for her, following her to Australia, for he was sure she would be driven to go home. He eyed her thin body curved over the red cushions opposite him in the *mafraj*; her intense face, her introspective, self-obsessed, slightly mad manner. He felt hollow with fear and indecision. For a brief moment he thought that he would have to leave for her to turn to him, and in that moment he found the courage to leave.

Lian picked up the sea story again in the lonely space
following Ibrahim's departure with a feeling between
yearning, nostalgia and dread. But Abdallah the Merman
stayed imaginary, gentle and crisp on the page and
caught fast in the net of sentence and phrase, dancing in
the formal cadences of medieval narrative Arabic. She
felt sane and sad but a vestige of the desire to be guided
by the story and to find her story in it tugged at her. The
hope that it would give her hope, and fortify her.
Abdallah of the Land's cooling wonder in the world
around him troubled her. Had this been true of her, too?
It is a fairy story, she told herself. It has to end well.

*Abdallah of the Land sat at the casement of his
friend's house, staring out at the street below.
When they couldn't see his legs, the passers-by took
him for an odd-looking Merman and greeted him
with the Peace. Small children swam idly behind
flocks of glow fish. Small fish darted in and out of
the windows, more bold than swallows. Fish-
children petted larger fish which swam like
deformed children among them. Across the chasm
a merchant displayed carved fish scalers and shell
ornaments in the shape of fishes for the tide of
customers who would flow past shortly. The house
opposite had hung out rows of fish to clean them in*

the currents. Smaller living fish were assisting in the process, flicking about with flashes of silver.

Abdallah of the Sea's young son appeared below, chewing on a fish as if it were a cucumber. Abdallah of the Land looked down at the eddies of hair around the boy's head. Fragments of the flesh of the fish he was eating drifted downstream in the current, only to be gobbled up by small silver scavengers. The child flicked his tail and disappeared into the chasm. Abdallah suddenly missed the smooth limbs and loud laughter of his children. These were fish, eating fish, living as fish. He suddenly thought that they must be cold to the touch and always wet in an embrace. He shivered.

That night he sat with his friend, talking as they had on the shore about religion and the important things in life. Abdallah of the Sea was thoughtful, and when Abdallah of the Land half-heartedly praised the culture and refinement of the undersea world, he shook his head and protested.

'We do not have what I would treasure most. We are cut off from complete fulfilment, for we can never make the Pilgrimage.'

'Don't you have Mecca down here?' Abdallah of the Land asked dreamily.

His friend the Merman looked up at him, his head on one side, his eyes amused.

'No,' he said drily. 'There is only one Mecca.'

The obvious nature of the Merman's problem
struck him and yet again he felt humble in the face of
his friend's purity of faith and purpose. Abdallah of
the Sea was looking at him.

'I would like you to do something for me. When
you make the Pilgrimage next year, could you place
a pledge of mine at the grave of the Prophet?'

Abdallah of the Land agreed, delighted to be
able to do something for his friend. The Merman
disappeared into the interior and returned with
something small and heavy wrapped in green shot
silk. Abdallah of the Land took it respectfully, and the
Merman cheered up and called his wife to bring food.
She served them a fish as big as a lamb stuffed with
smaller salty fish. The Merman's little girl shooed the
scavenger fish from the open window and Abdallah of
the Land looked at the fish on the table without
hunger.

The next day, just as they were leaving the house
to make the final swim to the shore, two Mermen
accompanied by swordfish rushed up and took
Abdallah of the Sea to one side and spoke quietly with
him. Abdallah of the Land overheard the word
'Lacktail' several times and his heart filled with dread.
His friend came up to him with an apologetic air.

'It is the law of this kingdom of the sea that
any Lacktail be taken to the King. I had thought
that we would slip by unnoticed, but sadly we must
go to the palace.'

Abdallah of the Land was as helpless as a child
thwarted. He had no choice, so he agreed with as
much grace as he could muster. The Merman was
crushed with self-criticism and seemed worried.

The palace was exceedingly splendid and covered
in glimmering jewels. All around it swam schools
of exotic fishes in brilliant reds, yellows, blues,
purples, tended by fish-herds. With their many
colours and exquisite movement they resembled
the birds in a garden surrounding a land palace.
They gave it a strange appearance, however,
for it seemed that the jewels were fishes and the
fishes jewels.

He was presented to the King in a hall
ornamented with mosaics of fruit trees. Topaz and
gold lemons and emerald pears and amethyst grapes
were figured amongst lapis lazuli branches. The King
looked him up and down and laughed and all the
courtiers laughed with him. Abdallah of the Sea
alone did not laugh. The King asked him his name
and his profession and found all of the fisherman's
answers hilarious. Then he asked,

'And what gift have you brought me,
O Lacktail?'

Abdallah of the Sea stepped forward and said,

'O gracious King of the Age. This Lacktail is my
friend and is here by my invitation. He has no gift
other than having saved my life.'

The King frowned. He was well aware of the rules

of hospitality. Then he suddenly cheered up and said,
'Well, in that case we must throw a feast in his
honour!' He waved his hand and servants scattered in
a swirl of currents and cross-currents. Before two
minutes had passed a great stone was carried in and
arranged with fishes of all shapes and sizes. The table
was built up to resemble a castle of fish, a difficult
feat, for they were very slippery. The King laughed
and the courtiers stared greedily. The King had
Abdallah of the Land seated to his right and Abdallah
of the Sea seated to his left and made much of
handing them choice fish with his own hand.
Everything seemed to give him great amusement.
He walked his fingers across the table, winked at the
Lacktail and eyed his courtiers and roared with
laughter. At the end of the feast he turned to
Abdallah of the Land and said, 'Because of the great
service you have done for the kingdom by saving the
skin of this minion, name your prize, and then we
will allow you to return home to the Dry and Dusty!'
and he laughed again.

Abdallah of the Land was overcome with
confusion. He couldn't think of anything else, so he
murmured something about jewels.

The King looked bored suddenly and dismissed
them. At the castle gate a giant shell filled with jewels
was thrust into his hands by a disdainful courtier
who shrank from contact with his skin.

Abdallah of the Land wanted to rush home.

Someone was torturing her dogs. Confused scuffling, yelps and growls came from below. Laughter, scattering children. Was she a time traveller who could not intervene? Who had a responsibility not to touch, not to meddle with anything she saw? Never become part of the landscape. Take nothing, leave no mark. She felt utterly depressed. Should the dog be tortured because she was an Australian? The crippled dog gave a yabber of impotent rage and fear and before she knew what she was doing she was at the little blue window screaming at the children below.

'Get away from the dog! Who are you? What family are you from? Oh ye lacking compassion! Git!'

Both dogs were cowering under a battered green sedan. The mother had been lunging at the children as they threw rocks at the cripple behind her. The children had been circling the car like a small pack, intent on flushing out their quarry. At the sound of her voice they leapt back and froze, looking up at the façade of her house. They were mostly between perhaps ten and thirteen but one was a young man with a little beard. Lian directed her house's invective at him.

'You man. You should know better. Get away from the dogs and don't come back!

She wondered what they would do. She had pushed herself to the threshold of insane bravery. They were still standing there staring at the house when she rushed from the casement, threw on her *balto* and *hijab* and clattered down the stairs. She could hear sounds as she cranked open the lock. When she stepped outside, the street was empty. The two dogs watched her from under the car, ears down, deferential. Shaking and sweating, she started to laugh.

She had become a defender of dogs.

The kids didn't torment her dogs again and their parents didn't come to ask what right she, an *ajnabiya* non-Muslim, had to tick their kids off. No-one came to ask what it all meant and to make her accountable. Her speech about cruelty to God's creatures backed up from the Koran slowly dissipated from her mind and she felt oddly pleased with herself.

ADRIFT

Ammat al-Rahman looked at her, sidelong.

'They are talking, Liana.'

'Who?'

'Everyone. Halima. My mother is very unhappy. I think her sisters and other aunties will visit you.'

'Rahmana, we are friends, Ibrahim and me. He is in America, and I am leaving too.'

'Yes ...' Ammat al-Rahman blushed.

'What?'

'Yemeni men are sometimes friends with Western women.' Ammat al-Rahman's voice was thin and uncertain.

Lian didn't know what to say. Ammat al-Rahman touched her arm, lightly.

'It's not natural to wait. You are twenty-four. And look at Abha.'

Abha's tormented eyes.

All the threads that bound these young women into the precise steps of the dance, which fixed their orbit as certainly as stars, were breaking. History, memory and centuries of experience guided Ammat al-Rahman's hands, for Ammat al-Rahman wanted no more than her mother and grandmother had wanted before her, although she wanted more than they had got. She was very young and made wise only by hope and by her mother's experience. She was happy as this season's flower on an ancient tree. Ammat al-Rahman could no more comprehend Lian's journey than she could have conceived of herself as the first, frail sapling in unknown soil and conditions. She was born to be loved, full and glorious. Abha's life-altering desire for education and freedom, more striking than the story of unprecedented stranger-friend Lian, had seemed to her the first mark of a slow tragedy rumoured in an ancient forest.

Lian knew that for Abha, unless she was given the bitter relief of prohibition, there was no turning back. But Abha's uncles were no longer sure of how to guarantee her happiness and Ibrahim had refused to censure her. They protested with silence and dismay but not refusal. Somehow, at twenty-nine and unmarried, she had already left her people and her family.

Two days before, Lian had sat opposite Abha in the elegant *mafraj*, let in by a silent Halima. They were alone.

'You are always so unhappy!' Abha had said.

Abha had just refused the offer of marriage from the

university's history professor to the horror of her family and, guessing from the eyes, her own. On the last occasion that Lian had visited her, the scholarship to UCLA had come through but not the visa. The long wait for approval was ahead of her, and after that she hoped to join her brother in the alien lands.

Startled, Lian wondered: *Am I?*

Then she realised that Abha meant *you plural*. She smiled, tired of resisting the generalisations. All around her there was only *you plural. You, they, we.* And yet she had never felt more singular. Abha sat with a fine white cloth wound loosely around her head. She looked like a bride, right to the fraught holes of her eyes. The eyes belied the calm form and the soft-spoken assurance of her voice. Outside was no place to be and she was now outside. She could not go back, because to have refused made her strange and frightening to those who might meet her and greet her from within.

Abha wanted advice about America.

'I know I will have to go with my face uncovered,' she said restlessly. 'It is not the same there. You do not understand covering.' She laughed. '*You* do, Liana. Westerners do not.'

Do I?

Abha stared at the wall. 'My face is my own. I don't want strangers to see it. It will take away my freedom.'

Then she said, resignedly, 'One must conform.'

Lian agreed that Americans would be repelled by the *litham* and would set Abha apart.

'I must, however, keep the *hijab*!'

Lian said that she thought Americans would also misunderstand the *hijab*.

'They need a clothes dictionary!'

'They have one.'

Abha stared at the wall. It was polished gypsum carved with verses. Her face softened.

'Can you read that?'

Lian read it with care for the cadences of recitation Arabic. Abha's beautiful face lit up.

'Do you read the Koran?'

She told Abha how she had read every day with her teacher, practising case endings and learning short verses by heart.

'I am not sure that you should be handling the Koran, since you are an unbeliever,' Abha said suddenly. She seemed jagged with fear and isolation, and sudden uncertainties were chafing at every breath.

'That cannot be right. If unbelievers cannot touch the Koran, how can they discover the path to belief?'

Abha looked relieved.

'Yes. That makes sense. I will ask my Imam about it.' The eyes were tortured again. 'But promise me, since you do read it with respect, promise me that you will not touch it when you are menstruating!'

Promise.

Abha twisted the soft white folds of cloth at her chest. Her breathing seemed to hurt her. A strange feeling came over Lian that the whole conversation had been about something else entirely. Abha needed comfort out alone in the cold dark interstices where she could be reached by no-one. Lian was experienced in this and Abha innocent but Lian could not have expressed it in words.

What could she say to Ammat al-Rahman?

'Her fate,' she said in Arabic, hiding behind the stock phrase. Rahmana's eyes swam with tears.

'Liana ...!'

Abdallah the Merman rushed Abdallah of the Land away from the glittering palace.

'We should hurry,' he said, 'You know what kings are like. He might change his mind and keep you as a curiosity and an entertainment.'

They swam rapidly through several dominions and past the outskirts of several cities all glittering and spread spangled like a great robe cast down on the floor.

Abdallah missed red. He thought that if he bled down here his blood would seep out and dissipate in an unnatural greeny-purple cloud. He missed food. Everywhere he looked hordes of fish swam by, great catches that he would have laboured a year as a fisherman and never even seen. The wealth of the sea sickened him. The beautiful breasts of the naked Mermaids repelled him and the colours on his friend's tail revolted him. He found himself questioning the morality of much that he saw and explaining

the deficiencies of his friend's world in terms of
their tails. Crippled by the need to remain wet
and slimy, they could not wear proper clothes.
Banishing criminal men and women to the company
of their own sex was outrageous, an offence to
justice. Marrying by private decision was a weak
and cheating way to structure a family. The naked
bodies all around would guarantee infidelities and
no legal bond was there to control it. Most of all
he found their eating habits unsupportable.
Everything that had struck him as interesting and
exciting and progressive now rang coldly in his
heart. Everything about these people could be
explained by the fact that they were really fish.

His friend could see that he was homesick.

She got a card from Ibrahim, written in English.

Lian. I am a fish out of water. I hate America. I would
rather read about Americans. They hate me. Can you believe
it? Especially the women. I am losing my mind.

Always

It was unsigned. Of course. She wished he had
written his name. She would have liked to imagine that
long-fingered hand sure over the paper, making his
name. He seemed to be evaporating. Nameless. Hand-
less. Something turned in her belly and she laughed.
She ripped his card up into small pieces. The world was
such a small marble.

He could try Australia.

They passed some people organising teams of
large toothed fish at the side of a cliff. Abdallah
of the Land asked dully what they were doing.
The Merman told him that they used these
fish to tunnel in the cliff face and make houses
there. Newlyweds making a home. Then, as
they rose into the pallid shallow water, they
passed a great feast in which merrymakers
were silently dancing, waving streamers and
feasting on fish arrayed in spirals on the ocean
floor. They had flowers, coral tiaras and seashells
in their hair.

'What are they celebrating?' Abdallah of the
Land asked, captivated despite himself by the
spectacle.

'That is a funeral,' the Merman replied.

Abdallah of the Land was stunned.

'Why do you dance and feast and act so joyous
when one of you dies?'

His friend stopped and stared at him.

'What do you do?'

'Naturally we grieve, and wail, and tear our faces
at the pain of the loss!'

Abdallah of the Sea was silent in horror.
Then he said, 'Do you not believe, as I do, that
there is no God but God, and Mohammed is
his Prophet?

'Yes of course. We recited the Fatiha together,
remember.'

'And do you not believe that when someone dies they go straight to the Garden to be with God?'

'Yes, but ...'

Abdallah of the Sea looked at him strangely, his beautiful face hurt and bitter for a fleeting moment. Then his face went as blank and alien as it had been that first day when the poor fisherman had hauled him flapping awkwardly from the sea. They swam on, reaching the shore in silence. Then the Merman held out his hand.

'Give it back. Give back to me my pledge!'

Abdallah of the Land handed the small bundle back, protesting but also angry. The Merman leapt up and dived without looking back. Abdallah of the Land swam to the shore alone and climbed out of the water. His body was heavy and felt cold in the dry breeze. He suddenly remembered that he was naked and hunted around for his clothes.

The next day Abdallah of the Land felt no anger, only grief. Every day for three years he went to the shore with a fresh basket of fruit and called his friend, but the reflective water stared back at him blankly, empty to the horizon.

She put the book down, closing it noiselessly. So that was the story. That was the end. For a moment she felt afraid that it had uttered all that was possible for her, for Ibrahim. For a moment she felt the rush of Abdallah's tail beating the current about her head, but it faded. The story might have lost its hold on her but she was still disproportionately depressed. That was how it ended. She felt bottomless. Sad and still and black as a night ocean. She had lost all her certainties and all her armour for this. And she could not even speak Arabic as though she belonged, nor would she ever, even if she stayed for her lifetime. She had thrown away any awkward belonging that she might have had. She had not been home to the Island and the sea, to Nev and Phi-Van, for four years now and all for this. She could not unlearn the unravelling she had learned. She could no more unlearn Arabic, the foster mother tongue that had shown her up and marooned her. Abdallah might have failed to love all he saw, might have yearned to return home, but there is no return because there is no forgetting. You cannot untransform. Unflower. And Ibrahim? Did Ibrahim know this yet? She could not bear to think of his return from America and could feel herself closing away from him in fear. *What if there could be no moment more? What if it was the one breath of air?*

Under the influence of the story, she could not imagine sustaining daily life with him, sustaining the real Lian she had once been with him.

There was a kind of angry pressure in Yemen, squeezing her hard, ejecting her. The outraged mother and the army of women had not yet rapped at her door but she could feel them, pressing about her, tightening. In some strange way she didn't care. It was as if she had already left, had never really been here. They were part of a dream through which a predawn wind was blowing.

Underneath the book lay her ticket and passport inside a yellow vinyl wallet. She stared at them, certain only, but not with longing. Neither the failure of Abdallah nor the detachment she felt *even here*, sufficed as a story, but they did tell her something. She had, sometime ago, in some untraceable moment, cut the line that held her to stories too and had pushed herself out into the open sea.

There was, in the end, something deadly about trying to belong.

THE BOAT

Phi-Van was alone in a boat. The boat was familiar in all its details: flaked white paint mottling the strakes, a small transom leak, oars made of driftwood. The sea was familiar too. Each wave made brief eye contact, each wave raised a finger to the forehead, nodded and slid away. Under the surface a school of fish streamed, with that glittering *fish me* flip, the same school she had seen perhaps every day of her life.

Phi-Van's face was altered. She sat in the middle of the boat, pulling the oars strongly, looking steadily down the wake and into the distance and the past. The water slapped and sizzled ceaselessly against the wooden sides. Her eyes were shaded and Lian couldn't see them. Lian stared at her mother's feet. They were sandalled, raw and blistered, but they were a young woman's feet, familiar.

The dream slid down a long, shot-silk lee, darkened into green and purple, and the boat was gone. Phi-Van was drowning. Her bone-white brow broke the surface in a glimmering velvet sea, once, twice, three times, her mouth huge and dark, a cavern with the minute waves rushing in, with a minute tumult, over and under her raging breath. Phi-Van then rolled backwards like a dancer, like an acrobat or a seal, and sank face first, her eyes huge and dark, staring at Lian without anger or frustration. Lian watched her swim into the darkness below but did not follow.

Can Phi-Van cross the savage, empty ocean to a midpoint where each of them is both nothing and new? Can she re-encounter the blue and rotting flesh, the blistering of body and soul, death and death again and again, and the great, sentient nothing of that cold blue eye? Can Phi-Van allow herself to think back across the endless ocean, ravel her life along its path and see her mother in the hour of her death, supine in a leaking hut? Can Phi-Van cast off from the tiny scar of earth and self to which she has bound herself for those long, desiccating decades?

Phi-Van lies in the expanse of white of a hospital bed. At the remote lip, she can see Nev's hand and that is something to aim for and she knows that when she wakes it will be there. But for now she just sees the miles and miles of flat white, flat white nothing getting bigger and bigger. The ocean is white now, not blue. She has sat still as still, holding her breath, for most of her life leading up to this point, this now. Lian is far away. Impossibly beyond Nev's hand. She realises and in a moment relinquishes, yet again, all torture. What she needs to relinquish is all guilt. There is a small, all-savaging vortex at the centre of this limpid white bed and it is sucking her head down first. She tries to whisper Nev's name but her mind is screaming *Lian Lian* as her scalp is pulled down down and away, twisting down the centre of a cord, and then her mind empties.

It was not the end at all.

Sirena's lined face softened.

'Silly girl,' she said gruffly and gave Lian a hug. Lian submitted, then surrendered, not to Sirena's unexpected warmth but to the need which burst in her own chest. She cried, because it was too huge a thing to be faced and comprehended, and because she had no other outlet for the turmoil inside her other than crying into this strong, bony chest.

'Cry, darling, cry. It happens, but no-one listens to advice. I used to tell the young ones to leave Yemen alone but it only made them the more eager. "Don't mix!" I said. I gave up. Mixed-race babies have hybrid vigour. You'll see. Look at mine!'

Sirena's doctor was the one who organised secret caesarians, adoptions and restorations of virginity. Lian wanted — needed — none of them. She was certainly pregnant. She was going to have a baby. She was going to be a mother in six short months time. She was an *ajnabiya*, a woman from the peripheral lands.

Nothing could yet make it real. *I am going to have a baby. Be a mother. I am pregnant.* Her only reaction was dizziness.

Sirena helped her for a week with rough chiding, plenty of food, some golden baby photos of her own children (all in university now in Germany), and no questions. At the end of the week Lian moved back to her own house on a tide of feeling stronger than happiness or rage. She had no control. Day and night she was charged with something bigger than herself, bigger than wonder or joy.

Everything had changed. For the first time, her ability to record an experience faithfully, to preserve, to savour, was a gift. It was as if all her life she had been preparing for this one experience; to know fully what this was and what it could mean. To know it and to feel it and to not be Phi-Van within it.

Everything had changed; and who would have thought that it could be so easy, so absolute, so shocking.

Everything had changed.

She lay in the white room reading the dictionary, reading the colours, her body vibrating with the sounds from outside. Many words she read she recognised from the story: here and there, dotted throughout the dictionary, was one of the small fragments that had been part of the whole thing but now could be anything. Each sound from outside passed through her skin as if it was water, through her bones, down, down to the centre. She was at the mercy of the words of the world. Every word in her head, every sound from her lips, every shriek from the boys outside, bark, clank of the gas carrier, call of the muezzin turned inward as if there was infinite space within her to house all possible noise. First her body had left her and now this. She could not feel bad, not just now. In the centre of all this flesh and bone was a something, inchoate, raw and hot. Inside her body was a molten core speaking of trouble, a maelstrom, speaking. Inside her was someone else, curled up small against the keel and strakes of her body. Inside her was something that said the absolute and final *no*. There was no life in Yemen now, for her, for now, maybe forever. She felt no grief. And then she felt the hot sweat seethe to the surface of her skin and a shudder of delight. She was afraid — this was love. All the noises gathered, rang out a morse code, a message danced out to America, to the Island, all the way back to herself. *Nev, Ibrahim, Phi-Van.* She felt her body dropping everything and rushing to help. She felt her chest expand to fit three in. She felt her spine stiffen to firmness and her ribs holding her, buoyant. She felt her mind slip from all hard surfaces, rigid faces, harsh words and wander off. Her body had taken over the world, had lost itself only to become absolute. Something that was both joy and horror washed and rolled through her, crashing and roaring. She was giddy and afraid.

What a disaster.

What a wonder.

She stood up and went to the wardrobe, Helena's sturdy Western single door. Inside the door was a full-length mirror. She swung it back and it picked up the coloured reds and blues from the window. She took off her *balto*, which was doubling as a dressing gown, and stared at this new, powerful body. She was lit from the front and behind by the windows and their reflections. Her shoulders were muscled with bony hooks protrud-ing at the ends of the arc of her wishbone, hooks holding her and pinning her in the flesh. Her breasts were sharp, conical, with a savage air, the nipples deeper red than she remembered. Her blood was rising on the tide and she felt a kind of river running and rushing through her solar plexus. In her belly was a globe as hard and round as a ball of string. Her ribs rose and fell, dipping under and out of the flesh like serried rows of mysterious oars. Yes, her body said, I have been here waiting for you all this time. She was lithe, curved, conical, sharp and full. She raised the left of those lovely arms and splayed the fingers. Infinite control. Infinite vigour and grace. She tensed and the muscles leapt blue and rippling at her biceps and forearm. Her hand was big enough to hold a head as one would a ball, her arm strong enough to throw it far out to sea. She put her other hand on her left breast and felt the nipple pierce her palm. Her hand throbbed and she closed it like a claw, but nothing could hurt and the marks of her fingers on her breast made her think of this body and sex. And for the first time, she let Ibrahim's shadowed eyes, hot and frank and young, rise in her memory, and felt again the warm hard muscle of his belly and chest patterned and fitting against her glimmering thighs and ribs and breast, felt the weakness and strength of desire. Nothing in her could turn it or demolish it. He fitted her.

She held all their histories and broken stories scrolled in her palm. She felt like a matriarch or a witch. She would cast her lines and she would weave Ibrahim's and Phi-Van's worlds with her body. She was Phi-Van's mother, grandmother, and time had not yet begun. She was lit up until all around her reappeared, illuminated, picked out of the shadows. She was phosphorescent. And she wanted Phi-Van with a kind of thirst or lust.

She picked up Phi-Van's last letter from the window-sill. It was crumpled and yellowed from the light, still unopened. There had been no letters now for a long time. The paper inside felt brittle. It was not the uncontrolled projectile diatribe she had expected. It had only three words, looking frail in the centre of the page:

Phi-Van Lian Neville.

She dressed and walked out the door. The dusty street, with its eddies of rubbish and fragmented plastic, fetid smells and the vista of mesmerising happy children, hot yellow dogs and laughing young women, rushed up to meet her. Her body was a mass of feelings. Aching for the heat of Ibrahim's skin against it. Aching at the core. Tingling and electric in a walk across Sanaa to the Bab al-Yemen. None of it had had anything to do with the city, this city, after all. All of it had everything to do with this city.

She walked briskly as the wind picked up. The intense Sanani sky closed over her, sizzling and unstable in its chameleon blue.

The last night in Sanaa she climbed the parapet of the Taj and stared out at the fairy-tale city. The city was blacked out, leaving ink pools in the moonshadows and

226

the winking lights of candles in nearby windows. The Southern Cross hung low and upside down on the horizon. Lian smiled into the darkness. She was adrift, alone, and her heart was light. She was moving with the wind and tide, a king tide, washing her home. Terrible things lay around her, waiting there to be thought, but she refused to think them. She watched the world with the sense of flying. She might be back here again, sucked under in a yawning ebb with Ibrahim, but now she wanted to find Phi-Van and lead her back to the sea.

The moonlight washed over the dome of the mosque below her, picking out the white words scrolled around its form. Where she had seen cold moonrock she now thought of eggshells. She held up a curved hand to the rim of the moon and knew that Phi-Van was waiting, every day, by the empty sea, standing with her bags packed neatly inside her head, ready but unable, waiting for the moment that would make the world her home again.

Lian knew that she would walk in and her mother would see it on her face. She was looking forward to Phi-Van's horror. That gaping hole would be her one chance. She would dive in and wrestle her mother to life.

ACKNOWLEDGMENTS

Many people played a part in the forming and finishing of this novel. They are Annette Barlow, Kirsty Brooks, Rose Creswell, Cécile Druey, Abbas El-Zein, Mariana Hardwick, Jan Harrow, Sue Hosking, Ivor Indyk, Gay Lynch, Christa Munns, Nathalie Nguyen, Andrea Saleem, Sabri Saleem, Roger Sallis, Tom Shapcott, Daniela Siebeck, Julia Stiles, Ulrike Stohrer, Mandy Treagus, Philip Waldron, Teresita White; and my teachers, particularly Amal Abou-Hamden, Khalid Melhi, Walid al-Mutawakkil, Abdallah Osman, Arwa Shamhan, and the staff and management of the Yemen Language Center, Sanaa. Andrea Saleem gave me ongoing support and a memorable trip to the Red Sea.

Research in Yemen was assisted by the University of Adelaide in 1996, ARTS SA in 1999 and Mariana Hardwick in 2000.

ARTS SA also funded a stage of the development of this novel.

Sanaa and its suburbs and surrounding regions are real but all characters, houses and the Language School in this novel are fictitional.